ROAD

TO

REMEMBRANCE

Copyright

For information contact:

Joseph Wainwright
Josephwainwright114@gmail.com
Instagram: Josephwainwright_author
X: @JosephWain39594
Facebook: @josephwainwright.2023
Website: josephwainwright11.wixsite.com/wheels

Book and Cover design by Safeer Ahmed

ISBN: #979-8-9902096-1-9 (Paperback); 979-8-9902096-3-3 (E-Book)

First Edition: July 2025

10 9 8 7 6 5 4 3 2 1

ROAD

TO

REMEMBRANCE

JOSEPH WAINWRIGHT

Dedication

Dedicated to those who have lost a love due to war.

TABLE OF CONTENTS

PROLOGUE

Last Letter

DTG: 251400TFEB67
I Corps Army Outpost
Near Que Son Valley
Quang Nam, Vietnam

THE AIR WAS THICK with sweat and smoke, the distant crack of gun fire a grim reminder that even silence in Vietnam could betray you. Sergeant Edward Smith sat hunched on an overturned ammo crate, the rickety seat shifting beneath his weight. His helmet rested in the spongy red mud beside him, half-covered in jungle dust and grime. His hands – scarred, calloused, and dirt-streaked – gripped a pencil and a wrinkled sheet of paper.

The page trembled as he began to write.

Dear Em,

It's morning here, though you wouldn't know it by the way the clouds sit heavy over the tree line. We've been here for what feels like months, even though it's only been a few weeks since we moved to this fire base. Time doesn't move the same here. Sometimes it feels like it's going backward. Or maybe that's just me.

Edward paused, tapping the pencil against the paper as he listened to the low growl of a helicopter far off in the distance. Dust kicked up around the tent flaps, and somewhere a medic barked orders. He refocused, lowering his head again.

I know I haven't written in a while. I guess I've been trying to figure out what I'd even say. How do you tell someone who knows your soul what war is doing to it? What it's scraping away, piece by piece. I guess the truth is—I'm scared, Em. Not just of dying, but of forgetting who I was before all this. Of becoming someone you wouldn't recognize.

A breeze carried the sharp scent of gunpowder and rotting foliage. It mingled with the metallic tang of his rifle lying beside him within arm's reach. The scent was part of him now, like the sound of buzzing insects or the nervous chatter of boots just barely old enough to shave.

He glanced around the perimeter at the rest of his unit. The others gave him space – they always did when he was writing. They understood the letters weren't just words on paper – they were his anchor, keeping him steady on the edge of the abyss.

I was thinking about the summer we turned ten. Remember when we built that raft with the inner tubes and tried to sail across Tucker Pond? You kept telling me it would work even though I knew it wouldn't. We ended up soaked, muddy, and covered with leeches. But you laughed the whole way home. You always could find the sunshine in a thunderstorm. I wish I had that now.

I envy you, Em. I always have, though I never said it. You were always the strong one. You could look a bully in the eye and dare them to blink. I'd stand behind you, thinking I was the protector when you were the one shielding me all along. If I had half your spirit, this place wouldn't feel so heavy.

He stopped, rubbing his eyes, the grit of sleeplessness grinding against his fingers. He hadn't slept more than two hours a night in over a week. Not since the last ambush.

I don't want to make this all about the bad stuff. There are good moments too, even here. Last night, Reyes snuck out a can of peaches from a care package and shared it with us. I don't think I've ever tasted anything so sweet. For a few minutes, we were back home. Just boys around a campfire, laughing about girls and football and how every one of us was convinced we going to marry one of the USO dancers.

But then shelling started in the distance, and the moment was gone.

A distant shout broke through the morning haze. Edward looked up briefly. A supply truck rumbled past, tires skidding in the muck.

He looked back at the letter, his expression darkening.

There's something I need to say, Em, and I hope you understand. I'm not sure I'll make it out of here. And I don't say that to scare you. I'm just being honest. I've seen too much. Felt too much. Something inside me is slipping—like the parts that made me me are rusting away with every firefight.

I'm not who I was when I when I left. That Edward was full of jokes and dreams and plans for a future and maybe a family. I don't know if he's still in here somewhere. If he is, he's buried under layers of dirt and noise and blood I can't wash off.

But I haven't forgotten you. Not even for a second. You're my tether, Em. You always have been. And when it gets really dark out here - and it does - I close my eyes and think of your laugh. Of how you used to sing while hanging laundry or chase me through the cornfields after we'd sneak Mom's pie cooling by the window.

That's the part of home I fight to remember. That's the part I hope never fades.

The paper blurred for a moment, and Edward wiped at his eyes, swearing softly under his breath.

They're talking about a new mission. Something dangerous. Nobody's saying much, but I can tell. I don't know if it's our last stand, but I feel something stirring. I think maybe... maybe this is my chance to do something that matters. Not for politics or generals or glory – but for these boys beside me. They're good kids. You'd think some were barely old enough to drive. If I can keep even one of them safe, then maybe this nightmare will mean something.

I don't want to die. But I'm not afraid of it anymore. I think that's what scares me the most.

Edward stared at the page for a long time, the pencil still in his hand but unmoving. Around him, the jungle pulsed with life and death in equal measure. Somewhere behind the tent line, a young soldier was humming a tune Edward didn't recognize. It sounded like home, in a strange and aching way.

He swallowed hard and pressed the pencil down one last time.

Promise me something, Em. Promise me you'll live. Really live. Dance in the kitchen, sing too loud, fall in love if it feels right. Keep going, raise a family if that's in the cards. But most of all – don't let this place take more than it already has. Don't let it take your light too.

You've always been the better half of me.

Promise me you'll never let go of that.

Love always,

Edward

He let the pencil fall and folded the letter with slow reverence, as if sealing part of him inside. As if the act itself would somehow keep his words alive, even if he didn't make it back.

Edward stood, the ache in his knees sharper than usual. He slid the letter into the thin, yellowed envelope and scrawled Emily's name across the front. "Smith Family – Galesburg, Illinois" was all he needed. Everyone in their town knew where the Smiths lived.

He walked it across the dirt-packed camp to a dented wooden crate nailed to a post just outside the makeshift operations tent. It wasn't much, but it was their "mailbox" – and as sacred out here as any chapel.

Edward hesitated. His fingers gripped the envelope tightly, unwilling to let go.

He took a breath. The jungle air filled his lungs with heat and dread.

Then he dropped the letter in.

As he turned to walk back, a voice rang out from the edge of camp.

"Smith! Gear up – we roll out in five," his commanding officer, Colonel Kelly yelled out.

Edward nodded, barely hearing the words. His boots sank into the red clay as he moved toward the gathering squad. He adjusted his pack and reached for his rifle, the familiar weight grounding him.

The letter was behind him now, bound for Emily - the only piece of him he could afford to send home.

He didn't look back.

Chapter One

Shattered World

10:20 AM, CST; March 7, 1967, Tuesday
Monmouth College
Monmouth, Illinois, USA

EMILY'S LAUGHTER MINGLED with the rustling leaves as she walked the cobblestone path of Monmouth College's campus, her friends flanking on both sides. Their conversation ebbed and flowed with the rhythm of old songs – familiar, effortless, punctuated by shared memories and inside jokes that drew amused glances from passing students. In these moments, wrapped in the familiar tapestry of collegiate life, Emily felt anchored.

"Remember how Professor Hanesworth wouldn't stop going on about the Industrial Revolution last week? I could recite his lecture in my sleep," quipped Sarah, rolling her eyes.

"Better than dreaming about steam engines and cotton gins," Emily replied, a wistful for the history they were living, even as it was taught.

Their path wound them closer to the dormitories, a daily pilgrimage so engrained it required no thought. But today, as the red brick silhouette of her residence hall emerged, Emily's steps faltered. Her father's aging sedan sat at the curb, starkly out of place among the swirl of student cars. Its presence was an anomaly, an unwelcome ripple distorting the smooth surface of routine.

"Isn't that your dad's car?" Jenna asked, following her gaze.

"Uh, yeah. It is," Emily said, the words catching over her tongue. She hadn't expected him; their visits were calendar-marked occasions, not spontaneous drop-ins. Their laughter faded. In its place came the pounding of Emily's heart, a discordant rhythm echoing louder with each step toward the waiting vehicle.

"Is everything okay?" Sarah's voice was laced with concern, mirroring the sudden tightness wrapping around Emily's chest.

"Must be," Emily tried to reassure herself as much as her friends, but the seed of unease had taken root, sprouting tendrils of questions she wasn't sure she wanted answered. Her father's car, steadfast and familiar, now seemed like a harbinger, its steel frame casting a shadow over the sunlit afternoon. "Maybe he's just passing through," Emily offered with forced optimism, but her words felt hollow, insufficient against the swell of apprehension. She gripped her books tighter to her chest, a makeshift shield against the unknown.

"Want us to wait with you?" Jenna offered, her voice soft. It felt like a lifeline tossed into the churning waters of Emily's thoughts.

"No, it's okay. I've got it." Emily attempted a smile that didn't quite reach her eyes. "I'll talk to you guys later, alright?"

"Sure," Sarah nodded, though her forehead creased with worry. The two friends exchanged a glance, silently communicating their reluctance to leave Emily to face whatever news awaited her alone.

As her friends reluctantly continued on, Emily's steps grew heavier, each one an echo of the normalcy she was leaving behind. She approached slowly, clinging for a breath to the hope that she'd misread everything. Maybe her father had come with good news or simply had to take a work trip into the town – her mind grasped at straws, desperate for any lifeline of normality.

But as she neared, the truth clung to her like the chill of approaching winter – the unexpected visit was no happy coincidence. It was a disruption, a crack in the facade of her collegiate haven, and deep down, she feared what lay on the other side.

Her father's frame, usually unshakable and unyielding, slumped against the car door. His coat hung crooked, unbuttoned in the chill. Emily's heart hitched at this aberration from his norm, as precise and groomed as the paths crisscrossing the campus green. The silvery streaks in his hair seemed to have multiplied, each one a marker of stresses she could not see. He peered out from beneath a weary brow, his eyes searching for her with an urgency that tightened her chest.

"Hey, Dad," Emily called out, but the tremor in her voice betrayed her growing anxiety. She watched as he pushed off from the vehicle, a motion that seemed to require all his strength. His next steps were heavy, leaving impressions upon the earth as if he carried an invisible weight on his shoulders.

Their eyes met, holding a conversation no words could encompass. A myriad of unspoken fears danced between them, each one a silent note in a dirge neither wished to compose. As Emily drew closer, his arms opened – a gesture so familiar yet rendered foreign by the palpable tension that radiated from him.

"Emily." Her name, wrapped in his voice, was a whisper caught on the wind. Then, he enfolded her into an embrace that squeezed the air from her lungs. This was not the brisk, reassuring hug she knew – the kind that said 'I love you' before rushing back to tasks at hand. No, this was a clasp that spoke of desperation, a plea sewn into the fabric of his worn jacket that pressed against her cheek.

She felt his heartbeat, rapid and unsteady, drumming against her own. With every thud, her concern mounted, stacking upon itself like layers of autumn leaves soon to be swept away. Emily closed her eyes and breathed in the scent of motor oil and aftershave – faint relics of normalcy in a moment suspended between what was and what could never be again.

Gently extricating herself from the confines of his embrace, Emily placed a hand lightly on her father's arm. "Let's go inside," she murmured, her voice barely above the crisp autumn breeze that rustled the remaining leaves clinging to the branches overhead. With each step toward her dormitory, her mind became an ever-tightening coil of apprehension. Why was he here? What could have unraveled so profoundly to bring him to her in such disarray?

Her father's presence was a stark contrast against the backdrop of youthful exuberance and ivy-clad buildings. Students bustled by, immersed in their own orbits, oblivious to the silent drama unfolding beside them. She felt eyes on her, curious glances that seemed to ask why the rhythm of her day had been interrupted by this unexpected visitor.

As they ascended the steps to her building, the familiar sound of her key turning in the lock was deafening in its normalcy. The door opened on the small sanctuary of her dorm room – photos, string lights, and soft clutter. A haven, now pierced by grief's shadow.

"Sit down, Dad," Emily offered, gesturing to the unmade bed, her voice betraying a tremor she couldn't quell. He moved slowly, as if through a viscous fog, and perched on the edge of the mattress. His eyes scanned the room, never quite landing on anything, as though he was searching for an anchor in a sea of uncertainty.

Emily sat across from him, hands clasped together in her lap to still their trembling. The silence between them grew dense, like the gathering clouds outside her window promising a storm. He cleared his throat – a gravelly sound that did nothing to pierce the quiet. His mouth opened, then closed, a mute testament to the struggle within.

She watched him, heart pounding in sync with the clock ticking on the wall, each second elongating into infinity. His next breath seemed to carry the weight of the world, and as he finally met her gaze, Emily braced for the tempest she knew was poised to break upon her shores.

His hand found hers, the familiar calluses brushing against her skin in a grip that sought to steady them both. "Emily," he started, his voice fractured by an invisible fissure. "It's Edward."

The name hung between them, a specter that demanded recognition. Her breath caught in her throat. Her father's eyes, those mirrors of guarded strength, now shimmered with unshed tears. "He's... He's gone, Emily." The words stumbled out, tripping over themselves in their haste to deliver their catastrophic load.

A cold shiver raced down Emily's spine, rooting her to the spot. The photographs on the wall seemed to mock her with captured smiles frozen in time, as if the world hadn't just tipped on its axis. "Gone?" she echoed, the word foreign and jagged in her mouth. "But how? I just talked to him last week."

"It was an attack on his unit," her father managed to choke out, the syllable cutting through the thick silence like a shard of ice. He reached for her again, but the room was already spinning, the ground tilting beneath her feet.

Edward – her brother, her twin, her compass – couldn't be reduced to a past tense, a memory, a hollow. Yet here she was, watching her father dissolve into a figure marred by sorrow, a man shorn of his stoicism. She wanted to reach out, to shake him until the words rearranged into some lesser tragedy, one where Edward would walk through the door any minute, laughing off their fears.

"Emily?" her father's voice cracked, a plea woven within it.

Reality shattered, and with it came the collapse. Her knees buckled, no longer able to bear the weight of a life suddenly bereft of its laughter. The floor rushed up to meet her, the carpet fibers blurring into nothingness as her father's arms encased her, his own body trembling with the force of his suppressed sobs.

"Shh, it's okay," he whispered, though they both knew it was the furthest thing from the truth. His hand stroked her hair, a gesture so achingly familiar it only served to fracture her composure further.

She clung to him – her anchor amidst the storm – as grief rose around them like floodwater. Both were seeking solace in the shared heartache. But even as he held her, his embrace spoke of the chasm that had opened up beneath them – a chasm where Edward's laughter should have been echoing off the walls of their family home, where his teasing should have filled the empty spaces of their conversations.

"Emily, we'll get through this somehow," her father murmured, his voice raw with the effort of remaining strong, even as his world crumbled too.

But in the shroud of her bedroom, amidst the remnants of a childhood she'd never fully leave behind, Emily could only grasp onto the shards of a reality now irrevocably altered. Edward was gone, and with him, a piece of her soul that she knew she would spend a lifetime trying to reclaim.

Chapter Two

Long Road Home

3:45 PM, CST; March 7, 1967, Tuesday
Monmouth College
Monmouth, Illinois, USA

THE CAR DOOR CLICKED SHUT – a small, mechanical sound that echoed with the weight of the day's grim truth. It wasn't just a door closing – it was the audible punctuation at the end of a sentence neither she nor her family had ever wanted to read. Emily sat motionless in the passenger seat, her gaze unfocused as the world dissolved into streaks of autumn colors and the flat grey wash of the highway. Trees lined the roadside like mournful sentinels, their leaves rustling in a language she no longer cared to decipher. Once, she might have listened. Now, their voices were lost to the quiet that had wrapped itself around her.

Her father adjusted the rearview mirror, catching a brief glimpse of his own hollow reflection before easing the car away from the curb. The engine hummed a steady rhythm, filling the void between them with something other than the weight of their shared grief. He drove with careful precision, every turn of the wheel and flick of his eyes a deliberate act of control. Yet his hands – calloused from years of labor – clung to the wheel with a white-knuckled intensity that betrayed the storm just beneath his weathered calm.

Emily's thoughts drifted, untethered from the present. A numbness had settled over her like a thick blanket, muffling the sharp edges of reality. The passing scenery slipped by – a tapestry of ordinary life, indifferent to the stillness that seized her own. It all felt surreal, like watching someone else's story flicker across the wrong side of a television screen. The vibrant reds and golds of fall felt almost cruel in their obliviousness. Didn't the world know everything had changed?

Beside her, her father cleared his throat. The sound sliced through the quiet like a knife. "We don't have to talk about it right now," he said, his voice as steady as he could manage. But Emily heard it - the subtle tremor, the fracture beneath the surface, a man holding back the tide by sheer force of will. She turned to look at him then, really looked, and saw the sheen of unshed tears glossing his eyes. He blinked quickly, swallowing them down like a soldier bracing for a battle already lost.

"Okay," she whispered, her own voice sounding foreign to her ears. The single word felt foreign in her mouth, a thin and fragile lifeline. But it was enough. A single syllable offered across the chasm of their grief – a single flare in the dark. It was all she had to give. It was all he needed.

They drove on in silence, the quiet understanding between them thick but no longer unbearable. It had become something else – an unspoken agreement, a new kind of intimacy born not of conversation but of shared heartbreak. Every so often, her father would reach across the console and gently squeeze her hand, grounding her with that simple human contact. She would squeeze back, drawing what strength she could from the solidarity between them, even as the hollowness within her deepened.

When they finally turned onto their street, the sight of home did not bring the usual sense of relief. Instead, it loomed like a monument to the life that had been torn apart. The front yard, once filled with laughter and summer game, now looked foreign – frozen in time while their world unraveled.

Her father parked and turned off the ignition. The silence that followed was unbearable in a different way – thick, final, suffocating.

At the front door, the key turned in the lock with a hollowness that echoed through Emily's chest. As the door swung open, a chill pressed in around her. The house that once overflowed with vibrant life – Edward's laughter, music, footsteps – now seemed to repel the very notion of warmth. The walls, once familiar, now stood like stone perimeter of a tomb.

Her mother drifted through the living room like an apparition, slow and unsteady, each motion tinged with uncertainty. Her hands – those gentle hands that had so often been busy with love, tucking in sheets, braiding hair, and cutting sandwiches into perfect triangles – now hung limply at her sides. Her fingers occasionally twisting the chain of a locket around her throat. It caught the light, a small glint of gold, as if memory itself were trying to stay visible.

Catching sight of Emily, she reached out, her arms trembling with earnestness. Their embrace was a quiet collision of sorrow, two souls clinging to each other amidst the wreckage of their hearts. No words passed between them; there was nothing language could offer against a loss so profound. Their tears soaked silently into cotton and skin, the shared ache of grief of a mother and daughter mourning the same boy.

"Mom," Emily whispered at last, her voice brittle in the stillness.

Her mother didn't answer. She simply nodded, eyes unfocused and glazed with the reflection of an internal storm. She turned away like a boat retreating and drifting further into a fog. Emily watched her disappear down the hallway, her heart clenched tightly in her chest.

Alone in the foyer, the full weight of the house settled around her like heavy wool. Her hand lightly trailed the wall as she climbed the stairs, finger tips brushing over the bumps of old paint, grounding herself in the familiar. The corridor was lined with photos – snapshots of joy frozen in time. Every smiling face was a sharp blow, a breath caught in her throat, a reminder of a happiness that now felt impossibly distant.

Her childhood bedroom greeted her with a familiarity that was both soothing and unbearable. She closed the door gently behind her, as if shutting it softly might muffle the pain that had followed her inside. The room was the same – a time capsule, unchanged and unprepared for a world without Edward. The posters he had helped her hang, the bookshelf lined with shared favorites, the twin set of trophies from summer camp games – they were all still there, untouched by the news that had fractured her world.

She sank onto the edge of bed, the mattress dipping beneath the sudden weight of her small frame. Wrapping her arms tightly around torso, she tried to hold together the shards of her soul splintering under the pressure of grief. Memories flooded her - bike rides down gravel paths, pillow forts, and whispered secrets in the dark. This room had once been the epicenter of their imagination, a place for dreams, a shelter from every storm.

Now it felt cavernous, too vast and hollow for one soul alone.

She buried her face deep in the pillow, its fabric still faintly scented of childhood innocence. Finally, she let herself break. Not with the silent dignity and restraint she had worn like armor, but with the raw shuddering sobs that shook her to the bone. Her cries filled the room, bouncing off the walls that once held only joy. In the honesty of that release, there was a strange kind of peace – painful, but honest.

When the storm of tears finally passed, she lay in the hush it left behind, her breathing shallow, her body spent. With trembling fingers, she reached toward the photograph on her nightstand – a relic of a past that now felt like another lifetime. It was cool to the touch, its weight familiar and sacred.

She lifted the frame with care and cradled it in her lap. In the photograph, two children grinned up at her from the past – Edward with that unruly hair and mischievous sparkle, and herself, pigtailed and sun-kissed, both perched side by side on their grandmother's picnic table. It had been a day of scraped knees and ice cream promises. A day untouched by sorrow, a day when the forever still felt possible.

She traced his face with her fingertip, pausing at the curve of his boyish grin. A part of her expected him to leap from the stillness of the photo, to wrap her in one of his bear hugs, to tell her everything would be okay. But there was no movement behind the glass. No voice. No warmth. Just silence.

Her eyes lingered, and in that frozen moment, the silence pulled her backward through time. She could feel his hand in hers, the echo of bare feet chasing fireflies through dusk. They had been inseparable – a two halves of a whole, bound not just by blood, but by an understanding that transcended words. Losing him felt like an amputation – only phantom pain remained.

Now, the room echoed, every corner holding the absence of him.

She hugged the photograph to her chest, the tears returning, gentler this time. They weren't just for the brother she had lost – but for every future he'd never touch. The birthdays. The graduations. The holidays. The long-distance phone calls. The children he would never have. A thousand lifetimes stolen in one impossible moment.

"Edward," she whispered into the stillness, her voice a broken melody, "how do I walk this world without you?"

No answer came, and she hadn't expected one. But something inside her shifted. Slightly. A movement so small it might have gone unnoticed. As the last light faded and the quiet deepened giving way to the tender hush of night, she remained on the edge of her bed, holding the photograph close like a compass pointing toward what once was. The room, the house, the world – none of it made sense without him. But she was still here.

And somehow, some way, she would have to learn to keep living.

Chapter Three

A Folded Flag

8:00 AM, EST; March 24, 1967, Friday
First Presbyterian Church
Galesburg, Illinois USA

THE DAY OF THE FUNERAL DAWNED gray and somber, the sky was overcast mirroring the immense weight of Emily's grief. Thick clouds hung low across the horizon like a heavy curtain, casting the world in muted tones of silver and shadow. In the distance, the limestone steeple of the First Presbyterian Church pierced the skyline like a silent prayer. Rain threatened but never fell, as though even the heavens held their breath in mourning, unwilling to disrupt the fragile balance of sorrow.

Inside the church, the sanctuary overflowed with mourners – family, friends, neighbors, and even strangers drawn by Edward's story. Black coats brushed against polished pews, the scent of lilies and roses mingling with aged cedar wood in the air. Faces, drawn and solemn, bore the marks of shared sorrow as the community gathered to honor a young life stolen by war. There was a stillness to the space, as if time itself had paused to make room for grief.

Emily quietly sat in the front pew, flanked by her parents. Her posture was rigid, hands clasped so tightly her knuckles were pale. Her mother gripped her hand with desperate strength, an anchor in the undertow of grief threatening to pull them both under. Her father sat silently on the other side, his expression carved from stone, jaw clenched, eyes forward, unblinking. The soft rustle of hymnals and shuffling feet barely registered in Emily's ears. When the pastor began to speak—of sacrifice, of duty, of eternal rest – his methodic voice rang loud and clear, yet each word struck like a heavy stone in her chest, echoing with pain and sorrow.

Her gaze remained firmly fixed on the flag-draped coffin, and yet her thoughts wandered aimlessly spooling out across space and time. She remembered the warm light of Sunday mornings as children, the feel of Edward's shoulder methodically bumping hers during sermons when they couldn't quite contain their laughter. She thought of whispered jokes and how they'd been reprimanded more than once by their parents for passing notes during youth group or bible study. Even then, he had a way of lighting up every room, every silence. The pew where they had once sat giggling felt cavernous now, suffocating in its emptiness. Her heart ached with the contrast – joy to absence, warmth to cold wood.

She didn't remember standing. Didn't remember walking outside. But suddenly she found herself at the graveside as the final rites were read. The wind carried the pastor's words, scattering them like leaves. Her heart beat louder than anything she could hear. The world had narrowed to the rectangle of earth before her, an open wound in the land.

When the honor guard approached, time slowed to a crawl. She watched their every movement with painful clarity – the snap of their steps, the measured grace in how they began folding the flag. Their faces were unreadable, masks of discipline, honor, and reverence. Each precise fold of the flag seemed to tighten around her chest, a ritual too sacred and too cruel to bear. In that silence, the weight of all that would never be – birthdays missed, milestones unshared – settled in her bones like winter.

Then came the bugler's cry, each note sharply piercing her soul. "Taps" cut through the silence like a surgeon's scalpel, low and mournful, trembling with the weight of goodbye. Each note wrapped itself around her ribcage and squeezed tighter and tighter as they were played. Her sorrowful tears flowed freely now, carving silent trails down her cheeks as she watched the casket descend inch by agonizing inch into the earth. With each descent, a piece of her soul descended with him.

The folded flag was gently handed to her mother, whose hands shook as she received it. Her lips parted in a voiceless sob, her whole body shuddering as though she had been struck by lightning. Emily's own legs wobbled beneath her. She gripped the arms of the people beside her, fighting to remain upright under the crushing weight of the somber moment. All around her, the world seemed suspended – silent except for the wind's rustling and the breathless stillness of those left behind.

The reception that afternoon passed in a haze. The house overflowed with casseroles, cakes, and people bearing condolences. Voices murmured in sympathy, arms reached out for brief embraces, but none of it relieved her. Emily drifted through it all like a ghost, her smile mechanical, her replies came automatic and hollow. Faces blurred, hands patted her shoulder, words were spoken – but none filled the infinite void. Time bent strangely, elastic and slow, every minute stretched too long.

When no one was watching, she quietly escaped upstairs, slipping down the hallway to Edward's room. She closed the door behind her. The silence on the other side was immediate and thick. The room was exactly as he had left it: bed neatly made, books perfectly aligned on the shelves, the scent of Old Spice and dust lingering like a memory that refused to fade. She stood still for a long moment, afraid that even the act of breathing would disturb the fragile illusion that he might return at any moment.

She cautiously approached his bed and sat on the edge next to the nightstand. Reaching out, her fingers brushing over the surface before finding the small engraved wooden box she remembered from their childhood. It had his name engraved on the surface. This was the same box he had guarded like a fierce dragon hoarding treasure. Carefully, almost reverently, she opened it. Slowly, she began to look through the treasure he had left behind, hoping to find a connection with him that would explain the world. Inside were fragments of his life – worn baseball cards of his favorite players, an old tarnished compass from his days as a Boy Scout, the stub from a Bob Dylan concert they'd snuck off to together one summer night, and the keys to Milly, his beloved VW bus. But beneath all of these treasures, nestled at the bottom, was an envelope. She reached through all the bits of memories and removed it from the box. Scrawled across the front in Edward's unmistakable handwriting was her name. Emily.

Her breath caught in her lungs. Her heart beating like rhythmic drum. She sat stoically on the edge of the bed, the envelope trembling slightly in her hands. Slowly, cautiously, but steadily, she unfolded the letter and began to read.

Dear Em,

If you're reading this, it means I didn't make it back, and I'm sorry. I never wanted to leave you or Mom and Dad with this pain, but I hope you'll remember that I believed in what I was doing. We don't get to choose every path we take in life, but we can choose how we walk it, and I want you to walk boldly, Em. You've always had that fire, even when we were kids. Don't ever let it burn out.

I've been thinking a lot about the dreams we used to talk about—the road trips we planned, all the places we wanted to see. Remember that time we spent hours in the library, poring over maps and travel guides, sketching out routes like we were explorers? We said we'd pack Milly and hit the road the day after graduation. I can still see the excitement in your eyes when we talked about it. You were going to be the navigator, and I'd be behind the wheel, driving us toward freedom and adventure.

I hate that I won't be there to take those trips with you, but I don't want you to give up on them. Milly's yours now, Em. Take her and go see the world. Go find the places we dreamed about, and then find new ones I never even imagined. Take pictures, write it all down, and carry a piece of me with you every mile of the way. Take that journal we started? It's yours to finish.

Most of all, I want you to live. Don't let grief steal the fire from you. Laugh loudly, cry when you need to, and love with everything you've got. You've got a light that the world needs, Em. Share it. Live the kind of life we talked about—the kind of life worth fighting for.

I'll be with you in spirit, riding shotgun in Milly, cheering you on. When you hear the wind in the trees or see the stars stretch out across the sky, know I'm there.

Take care of Mom and Dad, and take care of yourself too. Promise me you'll keep going, no matter what. That's what makes you Em, my sister and the strongest person I know.

I love you, Em. Always have, always will.

Edward

Emily's tears soaked the pages as she pressed the letter to her heart. The words were like balm and blade, comfort and agony intertwined. In Edward's voice, she heard not only his love and dreams, but his belief in her – a belief she wasn't sure she could carry. Yet something flickered inside her, faint and fragile. It wasn't strength, not yet. But maybe the start of it.

*****

That night, she quietly lay awake in bed, unable to sleep. The letter rested on her nightstand, Edward's words echoing like a quiet drumbeat in her chest. Every sentence pulsed with challenge, with calling. She intently stared at the ceiling, eyes wide, heart raw. Finally, just before dawn, she rose. Barefoot, silent, she slipped down the stairs.

In the garage, Milly sat in shadow - a relic, a promise. Emily ran her hands along the chipped paint, the rusted edges, the faded stickers on the back bumper. She climbed into the driver's seat, heart pounding. The scent of the old upholstery, woven with Edward's spirit, clung to her like a memory. From the glovebox, she pulled out the travel journal – the one they had started together in high school, filled with dreams and destinations. She flipped through its pages: rough sketches of landmarks, scribbled lists, half-planned routes. In every line, Edward's spirit lingered. Here, she felt closest to him.

She sat for a long time, her fingers resting on the worn leather cover. Dawn crept into the garage, bathing Milly in a golden light. Emily didn't know what would come next. She didn't know how long it would take, or if she'd have the strength. But for the first time in days, she felt a direction, however fragile. A beginning, seeded in grief and watered by memory.

She turned the key. Milly's engine sputtered, coughed - then roared to life like an old friend waking from slumber. Emily smiled through tears. Edward's voice echoed in her mind.

Take pictures, write it all down, and carry a piece of me with you every mile of the way.

She would. And she would begin tomorrow.

Chapter Four

Breadcrumbs of Memories

8:00 AM, EST; March 31, 1967, Thursday
Smith Family Home
Galesburg, Illinois USA

THE WALLS OF EMILY'S ROOM HELD ECHOES of her grief, like a lingering smoke scent long after the flames had died. Light slipped through pale curtains, brushing against framed photos, a leaning stack of sympathy cards, and the neatly folded American flag resting in solemn stillness on the living room mantle. Dust danced in the sunbeams, untouched, as if no one dared disrupt the sorrow steeped into the space. Weeks had passed since Edward's funeral, but the weight of loss hadn't lifted. It had only settled deeper, woven into the wallpaper and floorboards like a second skin. Grief lingered in the hallways, tucked into corners like shadows that refused to leave. And in the silences, it felt as though the house itself was holding its breath.

Emily's days blurred together in slow motion. She moved through them quietly, like a ghost in her own home, unable to sit too long in one room without feeling overwhelmed by memories. The once-familiar rhythm of everyday life had become foreign, like trying to step back into a dream that no longer fit. She often found herself pausing outside Edward's bedroom door, fingers grazing the frame, heart hammering with both dread and longing. His scent clung faintly to the pillow, his guitar leaned against the wall, strings slightly out of tune. She wasn't ready to pack anything away. She didn't know if she ever would be. To touch his things felt like touching a wound, raw and sacred.

But something shifted the morning her journey began. She rose before the birds stirred, and wandered into the garage, where a shaft of sunlight struck the windshield of the old VW bus. Milly. Edward had christened her after their great-aunt Mildred, whose fiery red hair and fierce spirit had always made them laugh as children. Emily stood still, motionless, her hand resting on the driver's side mirror, heart thudding quietly in her chest. The van was weathered now – faded blue skin with rust creeping along the seams – but to her, it was sacred. It was a piece of Edward that still breathed, groaned, sputtered, and sometimes outright refused to cooperate. But it had carried his dreams. And now, it would carry hers.

The idea for the journey had started quietly, almost guiltily. She'd pulled Edward's journal from the nightstand again and again, fingers tracing the loops and curves of his handwriting – lists of towns, national parks, roadside diners, places he'd circled on gas station maps with smudged blue ink. Each scribble carried the cadence of his voice, the spark of his curiosity, and an echo of the laughter they used to share.

- *Need to see the Rockies. Route 66 for sure.*
- *Heard the Grand Canyon will make you cry.*
- *Must try banana cream pie in Missouri.*

The words became more than entries – they became breadcrumbs scattered through time, guiding her forward, nudging her toward the version of herself that Edward had always believed in.

Convincing her parents hadn't been easy. Her mother had sat across from her at the kitchen table, eyes rimmed red, worry etched deep into her face, fingers nervously toying with the edge of a napkin.

"Alone?" she whispered. "Emily, I just lost one child. I can't bear the thought of losing another. And what about school!"

Her father, silent at first, picked up Edward's journal and slowly turned the pages, his thumb pausing on a dog-eared corner with a smudged sketch of the Pacific coast. Finally, he looked up, meeting Emily's gaze – eyes shadowed with the ache of letting go.

"He would've wanted this," he said gently to his wife and daughter. "And you need this. Just… call us often. And send post cards of everywhere you go. Promise me that."

She nodded, throat tight, a thousand words she couldn't say pressing behind her lips, fighting for space with tears.

And so, with Milly loaded with a modest stash of clothes, his old guitar, his journal, a few Polaroids tied together with a string, and his old sleeping bag and mat rolled tight behind the passenger seat, she hit the road. The pines disappeared behind her as the sun climbed into a pale blue sky, warm and unfamiliar. She didn't have a rigid plan – just Edward's notes, the maps he'd marked, and a growing resolve to see the world through his eyes. She let the wind guide her, and for the first time in weeks, she felt like she could breathe.

The first few days tested her in every way. Milly's gearshift stuck stubbornly, often forcing her to pull over, yank at it in frustration, and mutter apologies to passing drivers. A tire blew on the morning of the second day, sending her heart into her throat and her knees to the asphalt. In Iowa, she pulled over at a sunflower field and stood still for a long time, letting the breeze press against her skin. In Kansas, she stopped at a motel with a broken neon sign and a kind old woman who left a paper bag of cookies at her door. Still, with the windows rolled down and a playlist of his favorite bands – CCR, Bob Dylan, Johnny Cash, and the occasional Rolling Stones track – she pressed on, dust in her hair and sunlight on her face, the journal never far from reach.

The journal continued to guide her, not just to places, but to moments. In a tiny Missouri diner with flickering neon lights and vinyl booths worn thin, she ordered the banana cream pie and laughed when it wasn't half as good as he had thought. In Arkansas, she slept in Milly beneath a sky so rich with stars it stole her breath – the Milky Way arcing overhead like a cathedral ceiling. And in Nebraska, when the air conditioner failed and the van began to overheat, a kind man named Gus with grease on his chin and a heart of gold fixed it without charging her.

"Hey little lady. You on some kind of pilgrimage?" he asked, peering over his glasses, wiping his hands on an old red rag.

She hesitated, then handed him the journal. "It was my brother's," she sputtered out between her tears. He read a few entries, nodded solemnly, and rolled up his sleeves.

"That boy must've loved you something fierce," he said, patting the hood after tightening the last bolt.

Emily stared at him, stunned. "He was my brother. He died in Vietnam."

"Still," Gus replied with a shrug, "that kind of love doesn't fade."

That simple gesture undid her. In the diner next door, she wept into a chipped coffee mug for fifteen quiet minutes before filling an empty page with a letter to Edward. She told him about Gus, about the surprise fix to the air conditioner, the pie that didn't live up to the legend, and about the way she missed his off-key humming in the shower-and his maddening ability to quote every line from The Adventures of Huckleberry Finn. She had told Gus that she figured this story is what inspired them to embark on travels of their own, to see the world, and never regret a moment of life.

As the miles passed, grief slowly loosened its grip. It didn't vanish, but it softened, like ice melting under spring sunlight. Each stop along the journey gave her a piece of Edward – and of herself – back. In Texas, she hiked to the top of a rocky hill he had once circled with the note "sunset here?" scrawled in the margin. She sat for hours at the summit, the horizon bleeding violet and gold, her fingers curled tightly around the journal in her lap, her heart aching and alive all at once.

The journal became her companion, her confessional. Page after page, she filled it – not just with letters to Edward, but with her own thoughts and reflections. She wrote about towns that surprised her, strangers who showed kindness, and the way she sometimes laughed at nothing, just because it felt good to remember. She scribbled recipes from diners, snippets of overheard conversations, and sketches of places she'd been. All pieces of a world that was welcoming her back.

The flatlands gave way to red rock cliffs, then to the white-capped peaks of the Rockies. In Colorado Springs, she wandered through Garden of the Gods, the stone spires towering like ancient sentinels. At a gas station nearby, an elderly couple noticed the military sticker on Milly's bumper and asked about Edward. For the first time, Emily told the story without tears. It felt like turning a key in a long-locked door, like letting fresh air into a sealed room.

By Utah, something had changed within her. She no longer felt like she was chasing a shadow – she was walking beside it. Each mile wasn't just a step away from home. It was a step toward healing, toward reclaiming the parts of herself that had gone quiet in the wake of loss.

She left notes at every stop, tucked them into the journal like breadcrumbs: pressed wildflowers from a roadside market in Colorado, a matchbook from a bar in New Mexico, a ticket stub from a Navajo art exhibit. She wrote to him like he was riding shotgun – because in a way, he was.

In Arizona, the desert opened before her like a revelation – red earth, endless sky. She took a photo of a rust-colored canyon at sunset and wrote beneath it, I found you in the silence between the winds.

Finally, late one golden afternoon, she crossed into California. The air changed – warmer, tinged with salt and eucalyptus. San Francisco rose before her, vibrant and sunlit, framed by the bay and bustling hills. As the sun dipped low, she drove across the Golden Gate Bridge, the wind tousling her hair as she stared at the endless water below, every cell in her body humming with something like peace.

She pulled off at a vista point near the bridge, climbed out of Milly, and somberly stood at the railing. The city shimmered behind her. Below, waves kissed the bridge's pylons. For a long time, she stood there, clutching the journal to her chest. Edward had never made it here. But she had. And in a way, so had he. In every mile, every stranger's kindness, every open sky and winding road, he had been there.

That night, she camped beneath the redwoods just north of the city. The stars blinked above like tiny, patient guardians. By flashlight, Emily wrote her final entry in the journey that Edward had started.

Edward,

I made it. I crossed the bridge you never got to see. And I felt you beside me the whole way.

You were right—the Grand Canyon almost made me cry. But the Rockies? They shattered me. And somehow, that was okay.

I'm still angry some days. Still lost sometimes. But I'm learning. You didn't just leave breadcrumbs for me to follow. You left me a map—not drawn in ink, but in love. In wonder. In courage.

And now... I get to choose the next road. I think you'd be proud of me.

I miss you every day. But now, I carry you in a way that helps me breathe.

Love,

Em

She closed the journal, the wind rustling the branches overhead like a whisper. She placed it next to an empty journal that she vowed to fill with her next steps of her own story. Somewhere nearby, an owl called out across the dark. She pulled her sleeping bag tighter, but for the first time in months, she felt warm.

The road ahead was still long, uncertain, and full of blank pages. But Emily was no longer afraid. Somewhere along the miles, she had begun to find herself again – and, maybe, begun to dream again.

Chapter Five

Doves and Hawks

2:00 PM, MST; November 05, 1968, Tuesday
Route 66 Starting Point
Flagstaff, Arizona, USA

THE ARIZONA DESERT STRETCHED WIDE and barren before Emily, the asphalt of Route 66 shimmering in the midday heat like a mirage of molten glass. Inside the van, the air was thick – laden with silence and dust – despite the windows rolled down and the groaning fan rattling on the dashboard. Sparse tufts of scrub brush and lonely cacti dotted the ochre landscape, broken only by the occasional sagging telephone pole or sun-bleached billboard advertising long-closed motels.

Emily's hands tightened on the wheel as she navigated the lonely highway, her mind a whirlwind of emotion and memory. Each mile felt like both an escape and pursuit – fleeing the unspoken grief that clung to her home while chasing something unnamed. She wasn't entirely sure what she was searching for. Clarity? Relief? A reason to keep driving east. Ever since Edward's death, everything felt hollow. The space her twin had occupied in the world – and in her life – was a wound that pulsed beneath her ribs, raw and unhealed.

Sometimes she still expected to hear his voice. To see his scribbled notes on the kitchen counter. To smell the familiar bitterness of his coffee in the morning. Instead, she had only silence and the constant hum of tires rolling over endless blacktop.

Up ahead, heat waves blurred the horizon, making it hard to tell where sky ended and earth began. At first, she thought it was a mirage.

But as the shapes materialized – two figures by the roadside, thumbs extended in the universal gesture of hope. Dusty and sunburned, their packs slouched at their feet, one of them leaning heavily against a fence post like his legs might give out.

Emily's gut clenched with instinctual caution. Her father's voice echoed, gruff and protective: Don't stop for strangers. It's not safe. Especially out there. But something in their posture – the weariness, the quiet desperation – made her foot ease off the gas.

She coasted to a stop a few yards ahead. The figures stirred, slinging their packs as they approached the van. That's when she saw the uniforms: Marines. Pressed but road-worn, boots scuffed, insignias unmistakable.

She rolled down her window, heart pounding. "Hey there," she said, voice hoarse from the dry air. "You guys need a ride? Where are you headed?"

The taller of the two stepped forward, relief flickering across his face. He looked about twenty, broad-shouldered, his smile easy despite the fatigue in his eyes. "Oklahoma, ma'am. If you're headed that way, we'd sure appreciate it."

Emily hesitated, glancing at the other man – slighter, appeared younger, standing a few paces back with his hands in his pockets. He wore a quietness that reminded her painfully of Edward in his rare, unguarded moments. Her heart cracked a little.

"I'm headed east," she said slowly. "Not sure where I am headed, Haven't been to Oklahoma yet. Hop in."

"Appreciate it," the tall one said. "I'm Luke, and that's Reagan."

"Emily Smith," she replied, forcing a smile as she unlocked the door.

They climbed in, grateful and polite, their duffel bags settling between their feet with the soft thud of well-worn gear. As the van rumbled back onto the highway, the silence fell – thick, uncertain. Emily kept her eyes on the road, unsure of what to say. But Luke's voice eventually cut through the quiet like a breeze.

"This old van's got character," he said, patting the dashboard. "She's got a name?"

Emily glanced sideways. "Milly. My brother named her after our great-aunt. Said she was tough and stubborn. The van, I mean. Well, both, actually."

Luke chuckled. "She feels like she's got stories in her bones."

Reagan, still gazing out the window, finally spoke. "The kind of vehicle you can trust when things get weird."

Emily smiled faintly. "She's never left me completely stranded. Just enough to keep me humble."

As the hours passed, the van filled with conversation. Luke was outgoing, quick to share lighthearted stories from training, odd camp encounters, and sarcastic impressions of their drill sergeant. Reagan, more reserved, offered dry commentary that made Emily laugh despite herself. There was something healing in their presence, something grounding.

They shared snacks had – crushed granola bars, a bruised apple, and a sleeve of stale crackers – while the radio sputtered between stations. Eventually, Emily gave up and handed over an eight track tape: Edward's road mix. CCR's raspy chords filled the space, and for a moment, it felt like the van held four souls instead of three.

By late afternoon, shadows stretched across the highway. They pulled into a roadside diner nestled between two rusting gas pumps. The neon sign buzzed faintly, promising hot food and cold drinks. Inside, the scent of fryer grease and burnt coffee hung heavy.

Emily noticed it right away – the looks. Not fleeting curiosity, but lingering glances. Some held respect, others unease. A few with open scorn. Luke and Reagan's uniforms, though dusty, marked them as Marines. And lately, that meant baggage – judgment born not just of war, but of politics, headlines, and protests.

Their waitress barely smiled, and conversation around them grew stilted. A man in a corner booth glared over his newspaper, his mouth pressed into a hard line. Emily felt her pulse quicken, the air turning heavy and sharp.

They ate quickly, avoiding eye contact. Emily's burger went mostly untouched, and even Luke's usual banter faltered. When they returned to the parking lot, the sky was painted in shades of burnt orange and lavender, the heat slowly ebbing into the cooling desert air.

She paused by the van, eyes closed, letting the breeze lift her hair. It was one of those rare moments where the world felt suspended – timeless and fragile.

But peace never lingered long. The first voice came from behind them, slow and cutting. "Well, well," a man sneered. "Look who crawled outta the jungle."

Emily turned. Several men were approaching from the far end of the lot. They looked local – jeans, sun-faded T-shirts, and the unmistakable swagger of boys who never had to prove their toughness because it had never been tested.

"Couple of baby killers," another one said with a smirk. "Bet you think you're real heroes, huh?"

Luke stepped forward, calm and unflinching. "We're not looking for trouble."

"Too bad," the leader said, stepping closer. "Trouble found you."

Emily's breath caught. The fear was immediate and primal. She knew what was coming. She opened her mouth to speak, to reason – but the men weren't listening.

The shove came fast. One of them lunged at Luke, it was like striking a match in dry grass. The scene erupted. Reagan moved fast, shielding Emily as fists flew. She stumbled back, hitting the ground hard, gravel biting into her palms. The sound of fighting filled the air – grunts, curses, the dull thud of fists meeting flesh.

"Stop it!" she screamed, her voice hoarse. "They're just boys – just like you! They don't deserve this!"

Her words hung for a heartbeat, but the attackers didn't flinch. One grabbed Reagan by the collar, yanking him backward.

And then – like thunder – came a voice that split the air.

"Enough!"

A chorus of revving engines roared into the lot. Bikers. Half a dozen of them, clad in weathered leather and riding vintage Harleys that sounded like war drums. The man in front, towering and broad with a beard streaked with gray, swung off his bike and stalked forward like a force of nature.

The attackers faltered. "We don't want any trouble," one muttered.

"Too late," the biker growled. "You made trouble. Now get lost."

The would-be aggressors scattered like leaves in the wind, scrambling for their truck and peeling off into the dusk.

Emily stumbled to her feet and ran to Luke, whose lip was split, bleeding and cheek bruised, but who was grinning through the pain. "I'm okay," he said before she could even ask.

Reagan leaned against the van, breathless but upright. A burly biker helped him steady. "Semper Fi, kid," he said, clapping him on the shoulder.

Reagan managed a faint smile. "Semper Fi, back at you." He noticed the unmistakable image of an eagle, globe, and anchor sticking halfway out from under the bikers sleeve.

The lead biker introduced himself as Mike. "You boys did alright," he said, surveying the lot. "But even Marines need back-up sometimes."

"We're grateful," Luke said. "Really."

Mike nodded once, then glanced at Emily. "You've got guts, girl. Not many folks would speak up."

She met his gaze, voice trembling. "Thank you – for everything."

Mike's gruff smile softened. "Take care of each other."

As the van pulled back onto the road, the last of the sunlight turned the desert to gold. Inside, bruises throbbed and silence lingered, but there was a shared resilience now – an unspoken bond forged in adrenaline and loyalty.

Emily glanced at the boys beside her. In their battered faces, she saw echoes of Edward. Not just the uniform, but the weight they carried. They were still so young. Still trying to find their way home through a world that seemed determined to break them.

And in that moment, as the desert wind streamed through the window and CCR crackled back to life on the stereo, she realized something: maybe she wasn't just driving toward closure. Maybe she was driving with it – together with these boys who reminded her of what Edward might've been, had he ever made it home.

Chapter Six

Flicker of Hope

7:46 PM, CST; November 05, 1968, Tuesday
Route 66
Santa Rosa, New Mexico, USA

THE ROAD STRETCHED AHEAD IN SILENCE, the kind that settled like a heavy blanket – thick, exhausted, strangely intimate. The adrenaline had long burned off, leaving behind a raw, quiet stillness that filled every crevice of the van. No one spoke. There was nothing to say – not yet. Wind whispered against the windows like distant static, and the headlights carved a pale, flickering path through the dusk. Desert shadows reached long across the land, soft and dark, like fingers stretching toward them but never quite making contact.

Emily sat by the passenger window, her forehead pressed to the cool glass. The temperature had dipped, and the smooth chill against her skin helped ease the pounding behind her eyes. Still, nothing could quiet the storm inside her chest. Her thoughts tumbled over each other like stones in the surf, sharp-edged and insistent.

She replayed the moment again and again in her mind – Luke's hand brushing hers. It had been nothing. A fleeting touch. But, it had been everything. Just the briefest of contact as they climbed into the van, a casual brush of fingers barely noticed at the time. But her skin had remembered. It had sparked, lit like a struck match in a dark corridor. Not just warmth – something deeper. Something that anchored her, held her in place when everything else threatened to drift.

Now, with the road unfurling before them and the scent of sagebrush curling through the cracked window, she stole a glance at him. Luke was at the wheel, hands steady, eyes fixed on the ribbon of highway ahead. His profile was carved in the shifting interplay of shadows and orange glow from the fading sun. There was a quiet gravity to him, something unshakeable that lived beneath the bruises and dust. A kind of strength that didn't raise its voice or flex to be seen. It simply existed. Solid. Unpretending.

Her pulse ticked faster before she could stop it.

There it was again: that flicker. That maddening, dangerous flicker – a flicker of hope. Not just for peace or healing. But for more. For something she'd shoved deep down for so long it felt foreign now. Not lust, not even romance. Just the feeling of being seen. Of not drifting alone in the fog of grief. She hadn't known how much she missed that until Luke looked at her like he had – like she wasn't just another woman in pain, but someone who still mattered.

They didn't make it to the next town.

By the time the last scraps of sunlight disappeared behind the copper-toned hills, the weight of the day had pulled them into a hush. No one said it, but all three knew: they couldn't go on tonight. Conversation had slowed to near silence again, lulled by fatigue and the weight of the day. The night felt too thick, the desert too vast. So Luke pulled off onto a flat stretch of dirt off the main road, the tires whispered across the dry ground and the darkness deepened quickly.

The headlights caught a crooked Joshua tree in their beam, its limbs twisted like a dancer mid-pose. Wind tugged gently at its branches, whispering lullabies in a language only the desert could speak.

They parked, unloaded a few supplies, and set up a small camp beneath the tree. Reagan found dry kindling and coaxed a fire to life, the flames rising quickly, eager for air. Luke and Reagan peeled off their uniforms and changed into faded jeans and threadbare T-shirts, the fabric hanging off them like loose memory. Emily tried not to watch, but her eyes betrayed her. Luke caught her gaze just once, and in that flicker of shared awareness, he smiled. Not teasing. Not cocky. Just soft, quiet, and full of something unspoken.

The fire's heat was a welcome against the cool night. Emily sat close, knees pulled to her chest, arms wrapped around them like a shield. The smoke stung her eyes, or maybe it was everything else – memories, thoughts, grief pressing down like weightless sand until she could barely breathe.

And then the words came – uninvited, unplanned, but unstoppable.

"Edward would've done the same thing," she said, her voice barely above the crackling of the fire. "He would've stepped in. Calm. Unafraid. Like he was made of steel."

Luke turned his head, eyes shadowed in the firelight. Reagan looked up but said nothing, giving the moment its space.

"Edward was your brother?" Luke asked, his voice gentler than she'd expected.

"My twin," she whispered. "We did everything together – birthdays, scraped knees, teenage rebellions. He always had this… quiet confidence, like the world couldn't shake him. Like if he was beside me, nothing could touch me. And then…"

She paused, her throat tightening. The fire cracked, and she watched a spark leap into the night sky and disappear. "And then one day he was just… gone. Like someone tore half my life out by the roots."

What followed came in waves. Childhood mischief, the letter Edward left in his memory box. The day her dad had unexpectedly shown up at school. Her mother's scream. Her father falling into a chair, silent and pale. She told them about the silence afterward, how the house became a tomb, every room echoing with the absence of his laughter.

She talked until her voice cracked, and still she kept going. Because the silence after grief wasn't peace. It was suffocation.

Luke didn't interrupt. Neither did Reagan. They listened – not with pity, but with presence. When she finally fell quiet, the fire had burned lower, the stars above them like scattered bone-white beads across the velvet sky.

"My cousin," Luke said softly, "died in a car crash. Drunk driver. He was seventeen. We used to talk about opening a surf shack in California one day. A stupid dream, but we meant it."

He looked into the flames, his jaw tight. "I haven't said his name out loud in five years."

Reagan shifted, brushing dust from his knee. "I had a friend who dropped during PT," he murmured. "Basic training. One second he was running, the next… gone. Heart defect. No warnings. Just… gone."

They sat in silence then, but it didn't feel hollow. It felt full – weighted with memories, shared loss, and the strange way pain makes strangers into something more.

Emily's eyes drifted back to Luke. The fire cast golden lines along his face, tracing the shape of his brow, his cheekbone, his jaw. She wasn't sure when his gaze had turned back to her, but he was watching her now. Not just with sympathy. With understanding.

He wasn't trying to fix her.

He was seeing her. Every shattered, jagged edge.

Later, after Reagan climbed into a sleeping bag and rolled over for some rest, he left them somewhat alone under the stars and the gentle snap of firewood, the silence stretched into something more fragile. More meaningful. Emily shifted closer to the flames, the warmth crawling up her arms like the ghost of a touch.

"I didn't think I could talk about him," she said. "Not without coming apart."

Luke's voice was barely above a whisper. "You didn't come apart. You're still here."

She laughed, though it sounded more like a breath. "Barely."

"I've seen barely," Luke said, turning toward her. "This isn't that. You're something else."

The words hit deeper than she expected. They wrapped around something small and flickering inside her and refused to let go.

"Why did you step in today?" she asked. "You didn't know me. You could've walked away."

Luke leaned back on his elbows, gazing up at the stars. "I saw something in your eyes," he said. "Like you were holding your breath. I know that feeling. Sometimes, when you're on the edge, all it takes is someone reminding you that you don't have to be alone in it."

Her throat tightened, and she turned her hand slightly, fingers grazing his. She didn't know why she did it – maybe she was testing the moment. Maybe she just needed to feel something that wasn't pain.

He didn't pull away.

Their fingertips rested together, quiet and still, and that was all it took. No kiss. No declaration. Just touch. Just presence. And in that fragile connection, something shifted. The ache didn't vanish, but it no longer consumed her.

For the first time in years, she wasn't drifting alone.

When she finally curled up in the van that night, her body bone-weary and her heart strangely light, she stared at the ceiling for a long time, the echo of his touch still tingling in her hand. Outside, the desert hummed with wind and crickets and distant night sounds. Inside, she let herself believe – tentatively, vulnerably – that maybe she wasn't broken beyond repair.

Maybe there was still something left to feel. Something real.

Chapter Seven

Scarred, Not Broken

11:21 PM, CST; November 05, 1968, Tuesday
Off Route 66
Glenrio, Texas, USA

THE VAN SAT IN STILLNESS beneath a deep navy sky, like a forgotten relic anchored in the desert. Its windows were glinted darkly, opaque mirrors reflecting the cold shimmer of the stars. Overhead, the cosmos stretched infinite and indifferent – constellations sharp and remote, like old wounds that refused to fade. The fire outside had long since dwindled to pale embers, its crackling voice silenced into whispers. Only the occasional shift of wind stirred the night, brushing against the van's metal skin like a sigh.

Through the rear window, Reagan's silhouette was barely visible, cocooned in his sleeping bag a few feet from the fire pit. His form rose and fell with the rhythm of sleep, breath slow and even, muffled by the thin veil of desert air. He claimed he liked the fresh air. That he slept better beneath the stars. But Emily knew the truth. He'd stayed out there to give her space. Space to think. Space to grieve. To think. To be alone – without being alone.

Inside, the quiet was too thick to be comforting. It pressed in from every side. Emily lay curled on the narrow mattress at the back, blankets twisted around her legs like ivy. The small space was warm – too warm – and every shift of her body only added to the discomfort. The fabric itched at her skin; the mattress felt too soft and too hard all at once. Her thoughts spun in tight, breathless circles she couldn't slow.

Her eyes were open, fixed on the ceiling, but she wasn't seeing it.

She was seeing him. Edward.

His boyish grin. The way his hair stuck up in the mornings, no matter how much water he slapped on it. How he'd hum when he was nervous, fingers tapping some phantom rhythm against his thigh. His voice – louder than hers, always laughing, always teasing. His arms around her when she cried: the skinned knee at five, the heartbreak at fifteen, the silence after he left at twenty.

She could still hear his footsteps echoing down the narrow hallway of their childhood home, the creak of his bed when he turned at night. He'd always said he'd keep her safe. Always promised he'd come back.

But he hadn't.

She squeezed her eyes shut, but that didn't help. However, now it was different. She was saw Luke too.

The image of him by the fire still clung to her – broad shoulders bathed in flickering light, his face solemn but steady, a quiet gravity radiating from him. He hadn't just stood between her and those angry men. He had seen her. And something in her chest still hadn't stopped trembling since.

The steadiness of his eyes. The rasp of his voice. The silence that spoke more than comfort ever could.

Then – a sound. Soft. Careful.

The van door creaked open, hinges groaning low. Her breath caught. She didn't need to look. She already knew.

Luke.

He stepped inside with the quiet grace of someone who didn't want to wake the ghosts. Ducking beneath the low ceiling, he moved soundlessly, boots left at the door, bare feet whispering across the cold metal floor. He was shirtless, the lean lines of his chest and arms etched in the moonlight. Scars and muscle. Tension and fatigue. A body carved from survival, not vanity.

He said nothing. Just looked at her. And waited.

She turned slowly, propping herself up on one elbow. Her heart kicked against her ribs – quick, uncertain, loud in the hush. A strange cocktail of longing, confusion, and something more primal stirred inside her. Something she hadn't let herself feel in so long, it almost felt like betrayal.

"You should be sleeping," she whispered.

"So should you,' he murmured, voice rough-edged and low.

He crossed the narrow space and sat beside her, the mattress dipping beneath his weight. His leg brushed against her hip – just barely – but the contact sent a jolt through her, sharp and electric. He didn't touch her beyond that. Didn't push. But the air thickened with tension, pulsing and alive. She could feel it in him. In herself.

She drew the blanket tighter around her shoulders – not for warmth, but as a barrier. Or a question. But it couldn't shield her from what had already stirred. Not from him. Not from this.

"I keep thinking…" Her voice faltered, then steadied. "If I let myself feel something good again – if I let someone close – it means I'm moving on. And I don't want that. I can't. It feels like… leaving him behind."

Her voice cracked on the last word, a hairline fracture that let the truth escape.

His expression shifted – not pity, but deep, steady understanding. He reached out slowly, deliberately, and found her hand. Warm and rough, his thumb traced the inside of her wrist with infinite gentleness. That small touch sent a shiver through her – not from cold, but of recognition. Of being seen.

"You're not leaving him," he said softly. "Grief isn't betrayal, Emily. It's proof he mattered. That he still does."

Her throat tightened, eyes stinging with tears – hot and unwelcome. She blinked them away, even as his words pressed down with unbearable tenderness.

"Edward was my twin," she whispered. "My best friend. We had our own language. Our own world. Half of me vanished when he died. I've been trying to live with the rest ever since."

Luke leaned in, closer now. His breath was warm against her temple. "Then maybe it's time to find the other half of yourself again," he murmured. "Even if it looks different now. Even if it's scarred."

A breath escaped her, sharp and trembling. Her eyes drifted to his mouth, and for the first time, she didn't look away.

"This doesn't fix anything," she said.

"I know."

She let the blanket slip from her shoulders.

And then they moved – together, without another word. Their lips met, tentative at first. A question, then an answer. A slow, aching kiss that melted months of silence. Her fingers found his shoulders and curled there, anchoring herself in him. The kiss deepened, breath tangling, shaped by hunger and restraint and something unnamed.

Luke groaned softly, a sound that made her whole body tighten. His hands slid along her waist, found her hips beneath the thin cotton of her shirt. She arched into him, gasping softly, as heat bloomed low and urgent in her. Every movement was deliberate, unhurried but intense – a reverent collision of need and desire.

Their clothing found the floor, lost without care. His skin was fire and steel beneath her palms. Scars mapped his back, each one a story she wanted to hear. Someday. Her fingers traced them like Braille, memorizing him. He kissed her neck, the swell of her breast, slow and worshipful. Each breath ghosted across her skin.

"You're real," he murmured against her collarbone. "You're here. And I need you."

Those words undid her.

She let go.

Of guilt. Of hesitation. Of the quiet terror that loving again meant forgetting.

She let her hands explore him freely, learning the contours of his body like a prayer. His breath caught as her fingers grazed his ribs, his hips. He kissed her again – longer now, deeper. Their bodies moved together, rhythm rising like a tide – slow, inevitable, full of silent urgency. There was no rush. No fear. No desperation. Just the careful unraveling of walls too long held upright.

He moved above her, strong and careful, the blanket soft beneath her spine. Their mouths met again, tongues tangling, fingers clasping. They were heat and friction and breathless release. They were two people who had nothing left to prove and everything left to feel.

And when it was over, when her pulse slowed and the ache softened into quiet, she lay tucked into the curve of his body, her head resting on his chest, fingers curled loosely against his skin.

Outside, Reagan's distant snoring drifted faintly through the half-open window. A strange, grounding reminder that the world hadn't stopped. That some things remained simple, even amid the chaos.

Emily closed her eyes, listening to his steady heartbeat beneath her ear.

She wasn't whole. She still ached.

But she wasn't broken beyond repair either.

And tonight – here, in the warmth of his arms and the hush of the desert – that was enough.

CHAPTER EIGHT

Bonds on the Road

7:30 AM, CST; November 06, 1968, Wednesday
Off Route 66
Glenrio, Texas, USA

THE NEXT MORNING, as the sun crept over the lip of the desert horizon, casting long shadows across the sand, Emily stood beside Milly and watched the world awaken. The sky was streaked in rose gold and amber – a slow bloom of light that kissed the land with reverence. A cool breeze brushed her cheeks, lifting strands of her blonde hair as if the wind itself were whispering a quiet benediction. The desert, in that sacred hour, was vast and hushed and wholly alive.

She tilted her face toward the warmth, eyes half closed, drawing in a breath that filled her lungs like a clean slate. The air was crisp and dry, scented faintly with dust and sage. With her exhale came a release she hadn't expected – a loosening, as though a long-held knot deep inside her had finally begun to untangle.

Behind her, the van's sliding door groaned. Luke emerged, bare-chested, rubbing sleep from his eyes and stretching until his back cracked. The gesture was casual, almost boyish, and it tugged a smirk from her. A moment later, Reagan crawled out of his sleeping bag, blinking in the morning light looking at both of them, rubbing his neat cropped hair, pulling a sweatshirt over his head like armor against the chill.

"Morning," Luke mumbled, voice still gravelly with sleep.

Emily glanced over, a softness in her gaze. "Morning."

She turned back to the horizon. "It's beautiful out here."

Reagan yawned, hands shoved in his pockets. "There's something peaceful about the morning. Like the world's still deciding whether it wants to wake up."

They stood in easy silence, watching the sun continue its climb. Then, wordlessly, they slipped into their quiet routine – breaking camp, rolling up sleeping bags, shaking dust from boots. Luke checked Milly's oil levels while Reagan organized their gear with a quiet efficiency. Emily packed up the food and water with practiced ease.

Soon enough, they were back on the road.

The highway stretched ahead like a ribbon of possibility, unfurling beneath the tires mile by mile. Fields gave way to valleys, valleys to plains, and all around them the heartland moved in slow motion – rows of corn swaying in the wind, red barns weathered by time, small towns that seemed untouched by the chaos of the world. It was like driving through a memory – part dream, part echo.

Inside the van, the mood had lifted. Conversation flowed more easily, laughter came more freely. The miles slipped by unnoticed – not because the road was short, but because the weight in Emily's chest had eased just enough for her to breathe again.

Luke filled the quieter stretches with stories from his childhood. He spoke of Oklahoma summers sticky with heat and joy, of riding old tractors through pastures, and feeding calves before school. He described the sweet scent of his mother's cornbread and the way his father always whistled while working. But mostly, the dream he carried of owning a small farm tucked away from everything. War had delayed it, yes – but not destroyed it. The way he spoke of it made Emily ache in the best way, like discovering a forgotten piece of herself in someone else's longing.

Reagan, more reserved, was slower to open up. But as the road stretched on and the van hummed beneath them, he began to share pieces of his world. He spoke of his siblings – how he and his father had fixed up the old home that his parents now lived in. For him it was a time that he grew close with his father and begun to understand some of the demons in his father's past. His voice carried the quiet conviction of someone who had seen too much too young, but still believed in second chances. He shared about his plan to go to trade school and restore classic cars. When he described engines and chrome, his eyes lit with a rare fire, as if he were speaking a private language.

Emily listened at their stories – sometimes laughing, sometimes just nodding. And when it was her turn, she found herself telling stories about Edward. Stories she hadn't spoken aloud in years – the sacred and the silly, the tiny details that made him real again, if only for a moment. She described their secret forts in the woods, their whispered codes, the way they could read each other with a glance. It still hurt to talk about him. But it hurt less when the people listening didn't flinch or look away.

That night, after they'd pitched camp beside a narrow, trickling stream lined with wildflowers, Reagan called it early and disappeared into his sleeping bag. The moon was climbing, pale and watchful, and the fire crackled softly in the cool air.

Emily sat on a blanket, arms wrapped loosely around her knees. Luke sat across from her – close enough to feel the warmth between them, far enough to respect the space she hadn't asked for but still needed.

For a while, they just watched the flames. Then, as if drawn from her without effort, Emily spoke.

"I don't let people in anymore," she said, voice low. "Not since Edward. It's easier to keep my distance. If I don't let myself get close, then I don't have to lose anything."

Luke didn't respond right away. The firelight played across his face, catching the shadows in his eyes.

"I get that," he said finally. "I really do. After my cousin died, I kept everyone at arm's length. It was like… letting someone close again was daring the world to take them away."

Emily looked at him, and this time she didn't look away.

"What happened?" she asked gently.

His jaw tightened, then eased. "His name was Jonah. We grew-up together. Best friends. We did everything side by side – school, football, summers on the ranch. He was the kind of guy who made everyone feel like they belonged. He had this big laugh – like thunder. The kind that made people turn their heads. I used to think nothing could ever touch him."

He paused. "But then the accident changed everything. Sometimes it feels like life doesn't care how good someone is."

His voice was steady, but his pain pulsed beneath the words. Not loud. Just honest.

Emily reached out slowly, her fingers brushing his. "I'm sorry."

He looked at her, and something passed between them – recognition, maybe. Or a kind of understanding only grief could offer.

The fire snapped quietly, sending a shower of sparks into the sky.

Inside her, something stirred. Not certainty. But the barest outline of hope. She didn't act on it. Didn't name it. But it was there, resting gently between them.

*****

The next day, the scenery shifted – fields gave way to low hills, the towns grew smaller, more intimate. They stopped occasionally for gas or food, to stretch of legs, to snap a photo. Each stop reminded Emily that the road had a destination, even if she wasn't sure she wanted to reach it.

By the time they arrived on the outskirts of Luke's hometown, the sky was a dusky lavender, and the horizon had softened into farmland and low fences.

"You could stay with us for a while," Luke said quietly as the van slowed. His fingers tapped the dashboard, nervous energy. "Just a few days. My folks would love to meet you."

Emily's heart kicked up. The idea tempted her – deeply. But the intimacy of it, the vulnerability it required, was too much. Not yet.

"I can't," she whispered. "Not yet."

Luke nodded, though the disappointment in his eyes was unmistakable. He didn't push. "Well, if you find yourself this way again… you'll know where to find me for the next two weeks."

They sat in silence for a moment, then Luke reached for the door handle and paused.

"Hey," he said, turning back. "Would you write to me? While I'm overseas?"

Emily moved closer and took his hand. "Absolutely. And you better write back. Or I'll come find you."

She smiled – soft, real – and leaned in pressing a gentle kiss to his lips. Brief. Honest. Uncertain. When she pulled away, his expression was unreadable for a beat. Then he smiled, and this time, it reached his eyes.

The goodbye came quickly. Emily hugged Reagan first, then Luke, the strength of his arms gave a quiet promise she didn't quite have words for. Then she climbed back into Milly, fingers trembling on the steering wheel.

As she pulled away, she glanced in the rearview mirror – saw them standing there, still watching her, still waiting.

The road stretched wide and open before her as a dust cloud kicked up trailing Milly. But now it felt different. It didn't feel like escape anymore.

It felt like return.

She wasn't just running from the past. She was driving toward something – uncertain, unnamed, but real. The ache in her chest remained, but it no longer hollowed her out. There was warmth again, however fragile. There was a way forward.

And for the first time in a long time, Emily believed that maybe – just maybe – she could find her way home.

Chapter Nine

A Change in Course

10:43 AM, CST; December 7, 1968, Saturday
Big Red's Gas-n-Go
Dallas, Texas, USA

THE ROAD CONTINUED TO STRETCH endlessly before her, its black ribbon unspooling beneath the steady hum of Milly's tires. The windshield framed a sky so wide it seemed infinite, but the freedom she once cherished in the open road had lost its luster. What had felt like liberation only weeks ago now echoed her loneliness. She had begun to shake the nightmare of losing Edward – but now, she longed for Luke.

It seemed odd that his entry into her world was only a few weeks ago, but now his absence ached like a bruise beneath the surface – unexpected, tender, and persistent. She hadn't meant to grow attached so quickly. That wasn't the plan. But she had. In the brief time they'd traveled together, she'd grown used to his quiet humor, his fierce loyalty, the way his presence filled the empty spaces she never realized were so vast.

Now, alone again, the highway blurred into sameness – mile after mile without laughter, without conversation, without the shared rhythm of another soul. Her thoughts clattered in the silence. Even music, once a faithful companion, only skimmed the surface of the ache she couldn't dull.

At a dusty rest stop beneath a blazing midday sun, Emily pulled over. Inside the van, the air was cool and still. Unsure of what to do or where to go next. She reached into her bag and drew out Edward's journal hoping for inspiration. The leather, soft and worn at the edges, opened easily in her hands. Page after page bore his distinctive sprawl – looping script, smudged ink, margins crowded with doodles: airplanes, mountains, stray lyrics, impossible dreams.

One page caught the light differently. Her thumb paused mid-flip. A passage halfway down drew her in:

"One day I'll go to Texas. Not for the food, but because it's a place where time settles differently. Uncle John always said the land remembers. I want to stand in the desert and feel the history in the dirt. I want to look at the sky and know it looked the same to the ancients, to the conquistadors, to the outlaws. There's something sacred in that kind of continuity."

Emily read the lines over and over, her eyes misting. Edward had always been the dreamer, the romantic. His fascination with time and history had often seemed silly to her when they were younger. But now, years later and light-years from the version of herself she used to know, his words struck a different chord.

Texas. Uncle John. The land that remembers.

She closed the journal gently, cradling it like something alive. Without overthinking it, she pulled Milly back onto the road and turned the wheel west again. She didn't know exactly what she was searching for, but maybe Edward had left a breadcrumb trail meant just for her.

The landscape and scenery shifted as she drove. Lush greenery gave way to hard earth, to vast stretches of desert, rust-colored cliffs, and mesas that towered like sleeping giants. The farther she drove, the more the world seemed to stretch – wider skies, longer silences, deeper breaths.

The town she reached didn't have a name that particularly stood out – just one of those quiet places nestled near the foothills of the Sangre de Cristo Mountains. Adobe buildings squatted beneath bright turquoise skies, and the pace of life seemed to move at half-speed. This was where Uncle John had come after the war ended. A middle school teacher, he'd spent the last decades of his life shaping young minds and walking barefoot in the red dirt Edward had so vividly imagined.

Emily found a small inn with whitewashed walls and a green door that creaked pleasantly when she entered. The innkeeper gave her a pleasant smile, a brass key, and a promise of strong coffee in the morning. Everything was simple here. Somehow, that simplicity felt like a balm.

She spent her first day wandering. The town had a quiet pulse, a rhythm that seemed immune to the ticking of clocks. Children laughed and played under sun-dappled porticos. Old men played checkers outside a weathered hardware store. An older woman painted in the plaza, capturing the light on adobe rooftops with bold, confident strokes.

That evening, Emily wandered through town and into the old town library. A small but charming one, nestled inside an old Spanish mission. It smelled of dust, sun, and paperbacks worn by many hands. Shelves leaned with age. Light filtered through high windows in golden shafts. Without thinking, she offered to help. The librarian, a sharp-eyed woman with glasses named Inez, welcomed her without hesitation.

In the days that followed, Emily began to settle into a rhythm. She shelved books, cataloged archives, and learned to navigate the tangle of regional myths and histories that filled the dusty volumes. At first, the townspeople were curious, wary about the out-of-town girl who spoke softly and asked a lot of questions. But soon, they began to open up and welcome her as one of their own.

Mrs. Alvarez, the widowed baker, began leaving warm empanadas wrapped in cloth on her doorstep with small handwritten notes: "For strength." "For remembering."

And Miss Herrera, the schoolteacher, invited Emily to observe her history lessons, where she taught children about the Pueblo Revolt, sacred earth traditions, and the value of stories that weren't written down.

Emily found herself drawn to the local museum – an old, white stucco building filled with artifacts from various time periods: pottery shards, military medals, railroad spikes, woven blankets, faded black-and-white photos of solemn families.

One afternoon, as she stood before a sepia photograph of a group of young World War II soldiers, a man's voice broke the silence from behind her.

"You're not from here."

She turned. An elderly man leaned on a cane, his frame thin but upright, his face creased like the desert earth. His gray eyes sparkled with quiet intelligence.

"No," Emily replied. "I'm just passing through."

"Most people are," he said, tapping his cane twice before taking a seat on a bench by the window. "But some of us get stuck."

There was something about him – his posture, his tone, the way he looked at the photo with a kind of reverence – that made her sit beside him.

"I'm Emily," she said, offering her hand.

"Calloway," he replied, shaking it. "Mr. Calloway if you're feeling formal. But everyone just calls me Cal."

They sat in silence for a moment. Cal's eyes drifted to the journal in Emily's lap.

She blinked, surprised. "It was my brother's."

"You hold it like it matters."

Emily swallowed. "It does. He died in Vietnam."

Cal nodded slowly. "Then I'm sorry, more than you know."

He gestured to the photo on the wall. "My best friend's in that picture. We were nineteen. Dumb and invincible. He didn't make it past the Bulge."

There was a quiet reverence in his voice, the kind that only comes from having walked through fire and survived it.

They talked for hours. Cal's stories painted pictures of frostbitten mornings in Belgium, of ration tins shared in foxholes, of letters that smelled like home and sometimes arrived too late. Emily found herself opening up more than she intended, sharing not only stories of Edward but also her own guilt – of surviving, of not writing more, of leaving behind people like Luke.

"Grief," Cal said gently, "means you've loved deeply. It's not the enemy – it's proof you've lived."

His words sank into her, wrapping around the cold corners of her heart.

*****

Over the following weeks, Emily began writing more and more. Not just letters to Luke letting him know where she was staying, at least for the time being – though those continued, eagerly awaited, tucked into her canvas bag until the paper curled and the ink faded from folding. She continued to send post cards home. Also, she continued writing in a journal of her own, filling pages with her memories of Edward, with conversations she overheard in town, with dreams she hadn't known she still had.

The desert mirrored her healing – harsh, yes, but also vast and full of quiet moments of unexpected beauty. Coyotes howled in the distance at night, and dawn painted the mesas in hues of lavender and rose. There was something sacred in that stillness, something Edward had understood before she had.

Every now and then, she would get a letter from Luke. His letters arrived on plain stationery with a military logo on the envelope, but his words brought color to her days. He described the chaos and rhythm of life – drills, pranks, brothers-in-arms. He asked about her days, her thoughts, what she was reading.

He never pushed, never asked too much, but his words always left room for more.

Then, one crisp morning as the first frost coated the edges of the inn's windows, the innkeeper handed her a letter at breakfast. She recognized the handwriting instantly – tight, neat, unmistakable. It was from Luke.

She excitedly tore the envelope open with trembling fingers.

Emily,

We got the news this morning—I've been granted a short R&R in a few weeks. It's not much, but it's enough time for a meet-up if you're willing. Reagan and I are headed to Hong Kong for a few days. It's chaotic, loud, bright—but I'd rather be there with you. I know it's far. I know it's sudden. But I had to ask.

I think about you every day. I'm not trying to change your life, Em. But I'd like to be part of it, even for a little while. We'll be there the first 2 full weeks of April.

If you say yes, I'll be at the pier on the southern end of the city, just after sunset everyday waiting to see your face. I'll be the guy wearing a stupid grin and hoping like hell you show up.

Love Always,

Luke

Emily stared at the letter, her pulse thudding in her ears. The words blurred, and she read them again. And again.

Could she do it? Could she close the distance – both physical and emotional – that had grown between them? What would Edward say? What would she say?

The desert had given her space to grieve, but it had also reminded her that love and connection, no matter how fragile, were still possible.

She stood, her hands trembling, heart pounding. And then, without a moment of hesitation, Emily began to hastily pack.

Chapter Ten

Bright Lights, Big City

8:23 PM, HKT; April 4, 1969, Monday
Wanchai Ferry Pier
Hong Kong, China

EMILY HAD NEVER SEEN A CITY like Hong Kong before. It pulsed with a rhythm that was both electric and ancient, humming with life beneath the glow of neon signs and the press of centuries-old stone. The skyline rose like a jagged heartbeat, buildings lit from within like lanterns guarding secrets. Sampans drifted across Victoria Harbour, their sails pale and trembling like ghosts caught between worlds. The city was all motion – heat, noise, scent but inside the quiet hotel room, it all faded to a blur.

Because in here, it was only him. Luke.

When she had seen him at the pier, standing tall in his uniform with that familiar tilt to his stance, it was as though something inside her realigned. He looked almost exactly as she remembered: broad-shouldered, clean-cut, devastating. But his eyes carried a weight she hadn't seen before. A weariness that clung to him like shadow. Not obvious, perhaps, to anyone else – but to her, it was unmistakable.

Her breath caught. Just looking at him hurt and healed her all at once.

They didn't speak at first. No rehearsed greetings, no small talk. Just the way he reached for her, pulling her into him like a drowning man finding shore. She wrapped herself around him – arms at his waist, fingers splayed wide across his back - and they stood there for a long time. Trembling, clinging, uncaring of who watched.

"I missed you. I dreamed of this. I don't know how to exist without you," he whispered.

In the taxi, their thighs touched. His hand rested on the seat between them, just close enough that their fingers brushed. Neither moved away. She watched him through the window's reflection – his jaw tight, his eyes scanning the streets not like a tourist, but like someone still in war. Even his silence felt loaded, like there were a thousand words sitting just behind his teeth.

In the elevator, he finally looked at her. Really looked. And her heart cracked all over again.

The distance between them wasn't just physical – it was made of memory, fear, longing and restraint.

It vibrated like tension in a live wire, waiting to either snap or sing.

Inside the hotel room, Luke stood by the window, his silhouette bathed by the city's glow. Hands braced against the sill, shoulders tense, his whole body spoke of effort – the effort of holding himself together. The view was breathtaking – towers lit like fire, the harbor freckled with boat lights – but he wasn't seeing it.

Emily set her bag down softly. "You're quiet."

Luke's exhaled, the sound catching halfway out. "It's hard to come back. Even when I want to."

She stepped behind him and rested her hands on his shoulders. He flinched – just barely – but it was enough for her to feel the tight coil of tension beneath her palms. He was all restraint and muscle and memory.

Slowly, he turned. Met her gaze. And though his eyes were tired, older than she remembered, they were still his. Still hers.

"I keep thinking about the guys still over there," he said. "About what I'll be walking back into. And what I'll miss… if I don't come back."

Emily's throat tightened. She lifted her hand to his face and cupped it, her thumb tracing the edge of his cheek. "Then don't waste this," she whispered. "Let's make it matter."

He didn't answer. Just pulled her into him, holding her like she was the last real thing in the world.

That night, they didn't just make love. They touched like people starved, like pilgrims returning and rediscovering sacred ground. Her blouse slipped from her shoulders and he caught it mid-fall, as if even her clothes deserved reverence. His uniform shirt resisted – buttons fumbled in his haste – but when his chest was bare, she ran her fingers over every inch of him, relearning the topography of his body. The scars, old and new. The slope of his collarbone. The line where muscle met memory.

At first, Luke touched her like she was something fragile. Sacred and Holy.

Then the hunger surfaced like an erupting volcano.

His mouth found her neck, her collarbone, the dip between her breasts. Every kiss was a declaration. Every touch left something behind. His hands traced the curve of her waist, the bend of her thigh, and her body responded as if she'd been waiting for only him. Starved, urgent and open.

She gasped against his skin, pressing closer, fingers gripping him tight. She needed to feel every part of him. "I don't want to forget how this feels."

"You won't," he murmured. "I'll burn it into you."

They moved together in rhythm, in silence, in a kind of raw, sacred desperation. He held her tighter when she moaned. She whispered his name like it was a prayer. He made her feel everything – her own body, his hands, their history, the pulse of something that had no language.

They laughed, too – startled, breathless laughter, like light breaking through storm. Moments when she cried without realizing it, tears sliding across his skin. And through it all, Luke never stopped touching her like he might never get another chance.

Afterward, tangled in sheets and silence, he pulled her close. His skin was warm, damp, solid against hers. The world beyond the hotel walls felt impossibly far away.

"I don't know if I'll come back," he whispered.

"Don't," she said, pressing her palm to his chest. "Don't say that."

"I think about it every day. The dirt. The blood. The things that won't scrub off. They look at me like I invented you. Like you're some fantasy I made up to survive."

She kissed the corner of his mouth. "But I'm real."

He nodded, slowly. "And that terrifies me. Because if I lose this – if I lose you – I don't know how to come back at all."

She shifted closer, her legs threading his. Her fingers stroked his jaw, his temple, grounding him. "Then don't lose me. Come back. Come home. To me."

His eyes met hers – clearer now, almost pleading. Filled with pure, raw hope.

"Marry me," he said.

She froze. "What?"

"Marry me. Not later. Not when everything's easy. Now. Because this –" He gestured to the space between them, their bodies still entwined, "– this is the only thing that feels real enough to hold onto. I need to know I belong somewhere. With you."

Her breath caught in her throat. She wanted to say yes. She wanted to scream it. Shout it from the rooftops. But something inside her trembled at what it meant to love someone this much.

"You're asking me to live without you," she whispered.

"No," he said firmly, voice steady. "I'm asking you to live for us. Even if I don't make it back. And with me, if I do."

Tears welled in her eyes. He reached up and brushed one away with the back of his knuckle, gentle as a vow.

"I need you to say yes," he said. "So I have something more than just survival waiting for me."

She answered with her whole heart and soul. "Yes," she breathed. "Yes, I'll marry you."

And when he kissed her again, it wasn't hunger – it was devotion. They made love once more, slow and sure, like each movement etched the shape of their future into muscle and bones.

Over the next few days, Emily and Luke surrendered themselves to the rhythm of the city and to each other. With Reagan often in tow, they explored the bustling markets, the serene peaks of Victoria Harbour, and the golden light that poured through the narrow alleys. They sipped milk tea from street vendors, wandered through incense-thick temples, and marveled at how the city shimmered with both ancient echoes and modern glint.

But it was in the evenings, when Reagan slipped off for some rest. Emily and Luke let the rest of the world fade. In the privacy of their room, they rediscovered the landscape of each other's bodies and the fragile corners of each other's hearts. They talked late into the night, not only of the past they had lost, but of the versions of themselves they had each become. Every glance, every touch was deliberate – a rebellion against time and distance. They clung to the moment with the desperate tenderness of people who knew that the clock was always ticking, and that what they had could never be taken for granted.

On the final morning of the last day, reality returned. At the airfield, the world felt too bright, too sharp. Heat shimmered off the tarmac in rising waves. Emily stood still as Luke adjusted his pack, his face unreadable behind his sunglasses. But when he turned to her, she saw it – all the words they hadn't spoken.

He cupped her face, kissed her forehead, then her lips. Then, with deliberate, exquisite care, he bent and pressed one final kiss over her heart.

"Remember this," he said.

"I will." She watched him join Reagan as they boarded the plane. As it climbed into the sky, she held her breath until it vanished into the clouds. Around her, Hong Kong moved on – bustling, alive, indifferent. But inside her, time had stopped.

Her hand drifted to her chest, where Edward's journal lay buried in her bag – and beneath it, her heart, now anchored to the man who had given her more than memories.

He'd given her a new name to carry. A promise to keep. A future worth waiting for.

Chapter Eleven

Penned to Her Soul

2:32 PM, CST; April 24, 1969, Friday
Smith Family Home
Galesburg, Illinois, USA

SEVERAL WEEKS HAD PASSED since Hong Kong. The vivid colors of the city had long since dulled in Emily's memory, like a dream slowly eroding in the morning light. But Luke lingered. His voice in her ear, his laugh bouncing off crowded market stalls, the warmth of his hand wrapped in hers – these memories replayed like an unfinished melody. At night, she felt his breath against her skin. Sometimes she jolted awake certain he was beside her. But the space next to her was always cold. Always empty.

The day the letter arrived, it was raining.

The world outside blurred behind sheets of falling water, mirroring the fog that had crept into her chest. She hadn't planned on leaving the house – had no need to. Her parents were at work, and she'd been avoiding friends. Everything felt too bright. Too loud. Too wrong.

The creak of the mail slot barely registered. It was the thud of something heavier than usual hitting the floor that caught her attention. She padded to the front door in her socks, blinking in the gray light.

There it was.

A large, cream-colored envelope. Her name written in neat, unfamiliar script. In the top left corner: a military insignia. Her heart began to race before she even touched it.

It was not Luke's handwriting.

Her hands trembled as she picked it up. Her mind screamed no, again and again, as she turned the envelope in her fingers, willing it to vanish. But it didn't. It stayed. And it grew heavier with every heartbeat, as though it carried the weight of the world inside.

She opened it on the kitchen floor. She couldn't stand. Her legs wouldn't hold her.

The words blurred as she read, hers eyes stinging. She blinked hard, again and again, forcing the lines to focus. The letter were signed by Reagan. Luke's closest friend.

There was an explosion. A roadside bomb. An ambush.

He hadn't suffered. He was gone instantly.

Emily didn't cry at first.

She sat frozen, fists clenched around the paper until the sharp edges cut into her palms. Her mind refused to believe it. This was a mistake. Surely Reagan had written the wrong name. Maybe Luke had dropped his dog tags. Maybe someone else had been mistaken for him.

But it was the second page that shattered her.

Reagan had included a few personal words – something he said Luke would've wanted her to know. That he spoke of her constantly. That her picture was tucked inside his helmet. That in his final week, Luke had talked of marrying her, buying land back home, building something real together.

That he said she made him believe in peace again.

That destroyed her. The words penned to her soul.

A sound tore from her throat – a raw keening cry that didn't feel human. She collapsed forward, clutching the letter, her body wracked with sobs. Pain surged from every direction – hot and cold, sharp and dull all at once. The screams that followed was strangled, desperate, the kind of sound that only comes when the soul cracks wide open.

Hours passed. Or minutes. Time lost all meaning. Her mother found her there, curled on the tile like a child, the letter clenched in her hands. She helped her up, but Emily didn't speak. Not then. Not for a long time.

For days, the house was cloaked in an unbearable stillness. The kind that follows tragedy. Her mother sat with her, brought tea, made food, offered quiet comfort. But Emily couldn't accept it. Couldn't bear the weight of kindness when her heart had been hollowed out, again. She had just begun stitching herself back together after Edward's death. Now she was unraveling again.

Milly sat untouched in the driveway. Emily couldn't look at it without choking on memory. The sound of the engine. Luke's teasing about the "possessed" steering wheel. Singing Beatles songs down dusty roads. Taking turns napping in the back during desert drives.

That van had been their sanctuary. Their adventure. Their love story in motion.

Now it felt like a tombstone.

She couldn't bring herself to open the door, let alone drive it.

In the quietest hours of the night, she sat by her window, rereading Reagan's letter. She traced each word with her finger, whispering Luke's name to herself as though it might bring him back. Sometimes she read aloud the parts where he'd said Luke spoke of her – those were the only pieces that didn't hurt like knives.

And then one morning the phone rang.

It was a few days after the letter. Midmorning. Emily hadn't planned to answer it, hadn't spoken to anyone beyond her parents. But something about the insistent ringing made her move. She picked it up, her voice barely a whisper.

"Hello?"

A pause.

Then, a woman's voice. Warm. Trembling. "Emily?"

She didn't recognize it. Her heart faltered.

"This is… I'm Luke's mother. Mary Gentry."

Emily froze. The name hit her like a slap – both foreign and painfully intimate.

"I hope it's okay that I called," Mary continued gently. "I got your number from some of Luke's friends. He said you two were close, and… well, Luke spoke about you all the time in his letters. I felt like I already knew you."

The kindness in her tone undid something in Emily.

She sunk into the kitchen chair, gripping the phone like it was the only thing anchoring her to earth.

"I—I'm so sorry," she said, her voice cracking. "I wish there was something I could –"

"There's nothing," Mary said softly. "Except maybe we can grieve together."

Silence fell. Not awkward – just full. Heavy with meaning.

Mary explained there would be a memorial service for Luke at the Gentry ranch in a few weeks. It would be small. Just family. But they wanted Emily there. Luke would've wanted it. They wanted to meet the girl he couldn't stop talking about. The girl who had made him smile.

Emily promised she would come.

After she hung up, she collapsed into the chair, chest heaving with a sob she had barely held in. The idea of seeing Luke's home, his family, standing beside the people who had raised him – it terrified her. She didn't know if she could hold herself together. And she certainly didn't know if she could hide the truth.

Because the nausea hadn't passed. And her body was beginning to change in ways she could no longer ignore.

She hadn't told anyone. Not her parents. Not even herself – not really.

The thought had haunted her since before the letter. A missed cycle. A day of dizziness she blamed on jet lag. The way food had lost its taste. The fullness in her chest, the weight behind her navel that didn't feel like grief.

She had seen the doctor in secret. Blamed the feelings on bad food. But the results were positive.

Now it lived inside her, this secret. This shadow of Luke.

At night, she rested her hand over her stomach, whispering to the silence, "He would've loved you." And she cried. Not out of regret, but from the aching unfairness of it all.

She didn't know how to tell anyone. Didn't know how to carry it yet – not just the child, but the reality of being bound to a man she would never see again. Not in this lifetime.

*****

The day of the trip arrived like a storm. She moved through it in a daze, folding the dress she would wear to the service as if it were made of glass. Her mother offered to come, sensing her hesitation. Emily accepted with a nod.

They barely spoke on the drive. The world outside the car seemed quieter than usual. Even the sun seemed muted.

Emily clutched Reagan's letter in her lap, fingers wearing a groove into the crease.

Somewhere along the long stretch of highway, the land began to change – flatter, wider, open sky spreading endlessly above them. A place that seemed full of history and silence. The kind of silence where someone like Luke could've grown up strong and kind.

Her stomach twisted with each passing mile. Not just with grief. Not just with nerves. But with the growing weight of what she carried inside.

She still hadn't told her mother. She couldn't. Not here. Not yet. The words curled in her throat like smoke, unspoken but burning.

"I don't know if I can do this," she whispered, her voice barely audible.

Her mother looked over briefly, then back to the road. "Yes, you can."

Emily wanted to believe her.

They passed a small green sign that read: Welcome to LeFlore County. Luke's hometown.

The name hit like a punch. She blinked fast, swallowing the tears threatening to rise again.

The closer they came to the Gentry ranch, the more the world seemed to slow. She stared out at the endless fields, the fences running like seams across the land, the outline of a barn in the distance.

Somewhere ahead was the house Luke had grown up in. Somewhere ahcad was his mother, waiting for her. Somewhere ahead, a final chapter of him lingered.

Emily placed a hand on her stomach, a motion so subtle her mother didn't see.

"Almost there," her mother murmured gently.

Emily nodded, heart pounding. She wasn't ready. She might never be. But she would go. Because Luke had asked her to wait. Because even though his voice was gone, his love still echoed. And she had something left of him the world didn't know about yet. Not yet. But soon.

Chapter Twelve

21 Guns

3:00 PM, CST; May 15, 1969, Thursday
First Baptist Poteau
Poteau, Oklahoma, USA

THE CHURCH CAME INTO VIEW, like a ghost rising from the past. A white-steeple silhouette etched against the fading hues of late afternoon. It stood quiet and still beneath a pale sky, solemn in its waiting. Emily sat motionless in the passenger seat of Milly, her hands folded tightly in her lap, fingers laced together making her knuckles ache. She stared ahead, unblinking, her heartbeat thunderous in her ears, though her expression remained fixed in practiced stillness.

Beside her, her mother drove in silence, both hands gripping the steering wheel as if the van might veer off course if she let go. Her knuckles had turned pale, her eyes never straying from the road. It had been that way the entire drive. No forced conversation, no soothing platitudes. Just silence – fragile, heavy, and honest.

As they turned into the church gravel lot, the tires crunched softly beneath them. Her mother broke the silence at last, her voice gentle, but weighed down by the unspoken. "You don't have to do this alone, sweetheart."

Emily didn't immediately answer. Her gaze remained fixed on the church doors ahead, their heavy wood carved and worn from years of opening for both joy and sorrow. Her stomach churned with dread and unspoken truth. She felt it, not as a flutter or a symptom, but as a constant ache – a tension between life and death inside her own body.

"I know," she finally whispered, her voice hoarse from disuse.

Her mother reached across the console and wrapped her hand around Emily's. Steady and warm. "Let's take it one step at a time."

Emily gave the faintest nod and opened the door. The air was brisk. She inhaled deeply and stepped onto the gravel, smoothing the front of her dark dress with trembling hands. Her boots crunched softly beneath her – each step small but weighted with everything she carried.

People moved around them like shadows – friends, neighbors, extended family, fellow Marines. Their voices were hushed. Eyes cast downward. Yet she could feel their glances – fleeting, sympathetic, some lingering too long. She followed her mother inside, grateful for her presence yet desperate to disappear from everything and everyone around her.

They took a pew near the back. Emily chose the end, needing an escape route, even if it was only symbolic. The church was familiar, yet distant, like walking through a photograph of someone else's memories. The stained-glass windows filtered the dying sunlight, casting fragments of red and gold across the floor. She thought about how they could have looked like angels on a happier occasion. But today, to her, they were just broken shards of light.

The organ began its slow, mournful hymn – the old Baptist melody, "In the Garden." Once comforting, it now sounded like a lament. Each low, lingering chord echoed the heaviness in her chest. Emily sat upright, unmoving, her face a mask of calm forged through years of concealing pain.

Her eyes stared forward, but she wasn't seeing. Not really. Not the polished pews, not the floral arrangements draped in blue and white, not even the closed casket positioned near the altar.

She only heard his name.

"…Luke David Gentry, United States Marine Corps…"

The minister's voice rang through the vaulted ceiling, and with it, the finality of death settled over her like a shroud. Luke's name, spoken aloud, didn't sound like him anymore. It sounded official, ceremonial, like something recited from a telegram.

Her stomach clenched hard, and her jaw trembled. She bit down on the inside of her cheek, forcing her expression still.

The last time she endured a service like this was for Edward. She'd barely able to process the words. She remembered how she'd clung to her father's hand, nails digging in until both their palms bled. She remembered the scent of flowers that had made her nauseous. The swell of voices trying to sing through tears. The silence of the car ride home, like being sealed inside a coffin with her grief.

That day had broken her.

But this time- it was different. This was worse. This way obliteration.

Because now, she wasn't just a sister mourning a brother. She was a woman who had loved a man with every part of her soul. A woman carrying his child, alone in a pew full of strangers who would never know what he'd whispered into her hair on their last night together, or how he'd pressed his lips on her skin during private moments when their souls and bodies converged.

She couldn't tell them. She couldn't tell anyone. Not yet.

Her hand drifted to her stomach absentminded, instinctive. Just a gentle, protective curve against the flatness of her abdomen. It was a small gesture, but it felt like an anchor in the storm. The child growing inside her wasn't visible yet, but it changed everything. It made every moment heavier.

She hadn't told her mother. She hadn't told Luke's parents. She had no plan, no script. Only silence.

They mourned Luke as a fallen Marine, as a son, a friend, a comrade. But only she mourned him as the man who would have kissed her bare shoulder in the dark and whispered about baby names and where they would live. Only she would carry the part of him no one else could see.

The minister spoke of duty and courage. Of sacrifice and service. Of a nation grateful.

Emily wanted to scream.

What about love? What about his laugh when she teased him? The way he cradled her face after their first kiss? The way his thumb always brushed the back of her hand when they sat close, like a secret promise?

What about the life he would never get to meet?

What about her – left behind with nothing but memories and a secret heartbeat no one else could hear?

Her vision blurred, and she blinked rapidly, but the tears wouldn't stop now. They slipped down her cheeks silently. Her mother noticed and gently pressed a tissue into her hand, squeezing her fingers again.

Emily barely felt it.

She looked to the front of the church. Luke's mother sat rigid in the first pew, her posture pristine, her face unreadable. His father sat beside her, stone-faced, the pain etched deep but unreleased. Emily saw it all – the pain that never quite made it to tears, the struggle to maintain dignity when the world was burning around them. She admired them for it. But she couldn't be that strong.

A Marine stepped to the front to read a final letter from Luke. A tradition, a final word from the dead to the living. His voice cracked once, but he powered through. It was full of loyalty and courage and messages of love to his family, advice to his brothers, gratitude to his fellow Marines.

No mention of her. No mention of the baby.

Of course not. He'd never gotten the chance. He had never known.

Her chest ached as if someone had tied iron weights to her ribs. She folded her arms around herself and bent forward slightly, a movement no one else noticed but that felt like the only thing keeping her from falling apart completely.

Then came the 21-gun salute.

The volleys split the air like thunder – sharp, brutal, final. Each shot felt like it tore into her skin, peeling her open. The first shots shattered the silence like a thunderclap. Sharp. Violent. Final. Emily flinched. The second made her gasp. By the third, she was trembling.

The sound reverberated in her bones, in the memory of opening the letter, reading the words, the sound of the phone ringing inviting her to this dreadful day. In the moment she had dropped to her knees in the hallway and clutched her stomach in desperation, fearing what the letter was to say before she read it.

Luke was gone.

The child she carried would never know the sound of his father's voice.

A sob escaped her lips before she could stop it. Quiet and raw. Her mother leaned close, wrapping an arm around her shoulder, holding her. Emily allowed it. But she didn't lean in. She couldn't.

Her grief was too big. Too jagged. Too solitary.

The folding of the flag followed. Another ritual, precise and practiced, each movement like a blade slicing cleanly through the fabric of her resolve. The young Marine who presented the flag to Luke's mother did so with trembling hands.

A bugle began to play "Taps," and Emily almost choked. The haunting notes curled through the sanctuary like smoke. She closed her eyes, willing the tears to stop, but they kept coming. She pictured Luke – not in uniform, not with medals or salutes – but in the way he looked at her across a campfire. The warmth in his voice when he teased her. The way his hand covered hers, firm and certain. The last time they made love – so gentle, like they had all the time in the world.

She hadn't known then how short that time would be.

When the congregation stood to sing the final hymn, Emily remained seated. Her lips didn't move. Her voice didn't rise. She had no song left in her heart. Only silence, and memory, and the tiny flutter of life beneath her hand.

When it was finally over - when the sanctuary emptied and the people began filing out – Emily stayed in her seat. Her mother didn't push her. She simply sat beside her, quiet and still.

Only after the last guest had left, only when the sunlight had faded entirely from the stained-glass windows and the organist packed away her music, did Emily rise.

She walked slowly toward the front, where the casket still rested.

She stood there, alone now, and placed a hand on the smooth wood.

"I'm so sorry," she whispered, her voice cracking. "I wish I could have told you sooner."

She closed her eyes, her palm flat against the casket.

"You would've been a great father."

The words broke something open in her, and a sob tore from her chest before she could stop it. She turned away quickly, covering her face, afraid someone might see.

But no one did. No one remained. Just her, and the child she carried, and the man she had loved. And the silence that wrapped around them all like a funeral shroud.

Chapter Thirteen

Pieces of Him

5:00 PM, CST; May 15, 1969, Thursday
Gentry – Four H's Ranch
Poteau, Oklahoma, USA

AFTER THE SERVICE, Emily hesitated outside Milly while the rest of the congregation trickled toward the family ranch for the reception. Her mother gave her a questioning look.

"Are you sure you're up for this?" she asked.

Emily swallowed, her throat tight. "I need to be there," she said, her voice unsteady and barely more than a whisper.

Her mother nodded, giving her hand a quick squeeze. "Then I'll be there with you."

They had rode in silence. Emily sat stiffly in the passenger seat, one hand clutching the letter Luke had written her from Vietnam, now folded into a soft square in her coat pocket. It was his final letter – delivered days after his death. She hadn't read it yet. Not fully. Not with both eyes open. Just pieces. Bits. Fragments.

The ranch sat at the end of a long gravel road and was just as Luke had described it: sprawling fields, a red barn in the distance, and a modest farmhouse surrounded by oak trees. Despite the grief, there was a current of warmth beneath it all. People hugged. Children chased each other. A worn-out radio on the porch played an old Patsy Cline song. This was Luke's world.

Despite the somber occasion, there was warmth here – a celebration of Luke's life as much as a mourning of his loss.

Emily and her mother stepped out of Milly. She took a breath that didn't quite fill her lungs and moved with the tide toward the house. As they passed neighbors and cousins, Emily exchanged nods, but each face was a blur. She barely crossed the threshold before the noise of the house became too much. It was warm and full of motion – hugging arms and tearful greetings from people who had always been names from Luke's life. It was kindness, yes. But it was too much. She stood awkwardly by the door, her body tense, hands knotted in front of her like she wasn't sure if she was allowed to exist here.

The kitchen buzzed with activity – the clink of serving spoons, murmured conversation. Plates of fried chicken, deviled eggs, and banana pudding covered every surface. Emily stood awkwardly, feeling out of place, unable to leave, and unsure where to go or who to talk to. She'd heard stories about everyone here, but that wasn't the same as knowing them.

Her mother gave her an encouraging smile. "I'm right here if you need me," she said before stepping into the kitchen to help.

A young man in his early twenties spotted her from the kitchen. He wiped his hands on a dishtowel and approached with an easy, lopsided grin that tugged at something in her chest. He had Luke's eyes.

"You must be Emily," he said, sticking out a hand. "I'm Josh – Luke's little brother. Well, one of them. But I was his favorite."

She took his hand, her own still trembling. "Yes. I'm Emily. Nice to meet you."

"I've heard a lot about you. Luke wouldn't shut up about the girl that picked him up while hitchhiking."

Her lips curved and cheeks flushed. "That was a crazy couple of days," she said thinking about those nights in the back of Milly.

Josh looked over his shoulder at the busy kitchen. "Want something to drink? Sweet tea or… I think someone brought lemonade."

"Lemonade would be nice."

He returned a moment later with a glass and gestured toward the hallway. "You want to sit a spell? It's quieter in the front room. Ma's got pictures of Luke set up in there."

Emily followed him down the hall. The living room was modest, warm, with old wooden floors and a big braided rug worn soft in the middle. Family portraits lined the walls – Luke at different stages of his life. One in his dress blues, smiling, arm slung around Josh's shoulders. Another of him on a tractor with a big straw hat, grinning like a fool. Baby Luke naked in a metal washtub.

Josh motioned her to sit on the couch. "I know it must be weird, being surrounded by folks who know him from diapers and school bus fights. But I want you to know, you're not just some girl he wrote about. You mattered to him."

Emily stared into her drink. "I didn't know how to come here and not fall apart."

Josh sat on the arm of a nearby chair. "Fall apart if you need to. That's what today's for. To mourn. To remember. To help him live on through stories."

A few beats of silence passed. The low hum of conversation drifted through the walls. Slowly, the tightness in her chest began to ease.

"He loved this place," she said finally, eyes on a photo of Luke and a golden retriever. He wanted to come back here," she whispered. "He said the air smelled like peace."

"It does sometimes," Josh said quietly. "Yeah. He used to say that it was the only place where he could hear himself think."

Emily clutched her glass with both hands and began to breakdown. "I don't know how to live in a world that he's not in."

"You don't have to figure it out all at once."

A few relatives entered the room, and Josh stood to help. "Take your time. If you need a breather, the porch out back's nice this time of day. Just holler if anyone bothers you."

Emily politely nodded and slipped through the kitchen, out into the hush.

The porch stretched the length of the house, overlooking a sloping field. Fireflies were just starting to blink to life, and the air was thick with honeysuckle and warm dirt. She leaned against the railing, letting herself breathe in the scent of a place Luke had loved. She needed air. Space. Distance from the noise.

*****

As twilight settled and the guests began trickling away, the porch lights flickered on. Emily stayed outside, drawn to the hush of the evening.

The screen door creaked open.

Luke's mother stepped out, wrapped in a faded cardigan, her hair pinned back simply. Her face was tired, but her eyes were kind.

She hadn't seen Luke's mother all day, not really. The woman had been a storm of hospitality – pouring tea, hugging neighbors, keeping the casseroles warm.

Luke's mother was shorter than Emily expected, with silver strands in her chestnut hair and deep creases etched into the corners of her mouth. Her eyes, though – those were Luke's. Clear, intense, unflinching.

She carried a folded quilt and set it over the back of the swing before easing into it.

"I wondered when I'd find you out here," she said, her voice low, lowering herself onto the swing. "This was Luke's favorite place in the house. Are you okay, sweetheart?"

Emily nodded, "I needed some fresh air."

"I figured as much." She patted the quilt. "Luke used to nap out here after chores. Said the breeze made the best lullaby."

They rocked in silence for a while, the creak of wood beneath them and the chorus of crickets filling the space between.

"I wanted to say something earlier," Luke's mother said. "But… some things have to wait until the noise dies down."

Emily nodded, biting her lip to keep from breaking down entirely. "He talked about this place all the time," she said finally. "I feel like I knew it before I ever came here."

"I'm sorry," she whispered.

Luke's mother shook her head. "You've got nothing to be sorry for." She put her arm around Emily, as she looked out over the fields. "It's a lot to take in, isn't it?"

Emily nodded again, Luke's mother smiled faintly. "He loved this place. It was home for him, no matter where he went." She paused, her gaze softening as she turned to Emily. "He loved you, too. I could see it in the way he wrote about you."

Emily's breath hitched, and the tears she'd been holding back began to fall. "I loved him so much," she said, her voice trembling. "And now he's gone. It was such a short time together, but I don't know how to do this without him."

Luke's mother reached out and placed a gentle hand on her arm. "You don't have to do it alone," she said softly.

Emily hesitated, the words she'd been keeping inside threatening to spill out. "There's something I have to tell you. Something, I haven't told anyone," she began, her voice barely above a whisper.

Luke's mother studied her for a moment, then smiled gently. "I know. You're carrying his child, aren't you?"

Emily's eyes widened in shock. "How did you –"

"A mother always knows," she said with a knowing chuckle. "I guessed the moment you stepped out of that van."

Emily let out a choked laugh, a mixture of relief and disbelief washing over her. "Was it that obvious?"

"Not to anyone else," Luke's mother assured her. "But I've raised four boys. You pick up on these things."

Luke's mother shrugged, deadpan. "What, did you think you could walk into a small-town funeral with tear-stained cheeks, swollen ankles, and a bag of saltines in your purse, and nobody would notice?"

Emily stared at her, mouth open in disbelief. Then, slowly, she began to laugh. It started as a quiet chuckle but grew into something bigger, something cleansing. Luke's mother joined her, their laughter mingling, and for a moment, the grief didn't feel so heavy.

Emily wiped at her tears, her hands trembling. "I didn't know how to tell anyone, I haven't even told my mother," she whispered. "I didn't want to take away from today – from him."

"You're not taking anything away," Luke's mother said firmly. "If anything, you're giving us all something to hold onto. A piece of him that's still here with us. A reason to breathe tomorrow."

Emily's shoulders sagged as she let out a shaky breath. "I don't know how to do this," she confessed. "Raising a child on my own. Without him – I don't even know where to start."

"You start here, by letting us help," Luke's mother said. "You and this baby are part of our family, too. And we'd like to be part of their life, if you'll let us. You are welcome here anytime you want."

Luke's mother leaned back and added a wry smile, "Besides, I already told the sewing circle tonight that you're pregnant, so the rumor mill's got a head start."

Emily snorted, nearly choking on her lemonade. "You what?"

"I guess there's no use hiding it now," Emily said when she could finally breathe again.

"Lord, no. And don't bother trying. That'll just make them more curious. Let them talk. Give them something real to talk about."

"I never thought I'd be pregnant at twenty-two," Emily admitted quietly. "Not like this."

Luke's mother reached across and took her hand. "Nothing about life comes quite the way we expect it. But you'll find your way. You're stronger than you know."

Emily's breath caught, the weight of her secret finally beginning to lift. "Thank you," she whispered.

Luke's mother squeezed her arm. "No need to thank me, sweetheart. We're family now."

They stayed like that for a long time – two women from different worlds, brought together by love and loss, holding on to each other in the middle of it all.

As they began walking back into the house, Emily glanced at Luke's mother with a small smile. "You really guessed the moment I got out of the van?"

The older woman laughed, a sound that carried a hint of Luke's humor. "Oh, honey, it was written all over your face. Now let's get back before your mom accuses me of stealing you away."

Emily laughed softly, the sound surprising her. And as they stepped into the warm light of the farmhouse, she felt a little less alone in the world, knowing she had a place in Luke's family – and that she and her child would always have a home.

Chapter Fourteen

Not Again

2:15 PM, CST; June 15, 1992, Monday
Smith/Jones Family Home
Galesburg, Illinois, USA

EMILY STOOD AT THE KITCHEN COUNTER, slicing sun-warmed tomatoes from the backyard garden. The rhythmic motion of the knife gave her something to cling to – a ritual older than grief, older than memory. Outside, cicadas sang their summer dirge, a low drone filling the stillness. The kitchen smelled of damp earth, aged wood, and the acidic sweetness of fruit split open. A box fan hummed from the hallway, stirring the curtains and lifting the dust, and somewhere in the distance, a freight train groaned past Seminary Street, bound for nowhere she wanted to go.

This old kitchen had seen everything – birthdays, wakes, laughter that shook the windows, silences that shattered hearts. She'd raised her son here, after buying her childhood home when her parents retired and moved to Florida. She planted the tomatoes just beyond the fence with his tiny hands beside hers. She'd watched storms roll across the sky, clutched the phone when it rang with news that tore her life in two. And now, in this sacred, ordinary space, the air seemed to shift. Heavy. Expectant.

The day was as monotonous as any other. Then the creak of the screen door fractured the stillness.

Emily looked up, not fully expecting to see her son, Luke Jr. It had been over two decades with him, but sometimes she missed the days when he was small – rushing inside in search of a Popsicle or a sandwich, his cheeks flushed, breathless from some new backyard adventure. She missed their occasional road trips in the old VW, Milly, visiting forgotten towns and quiet trails, or summer journeys to his grandparents' ranch in Oklahoma. But now – he stood grown, graduated from college and ready to face the world. A man with his father's eyes and his father's posture, paused in the doorway like he didn't know whether to come in or run.

There was something in the way he stood – shoulders drawn, hands fidgeting – that pulled her heart into her throat.

She paused, hands stained red from tomatoes, the blade resting beside the cutting board.

"Something on your mind?" she asked, her voice calm, though her gut clenched. She dried her hands on a dishtowel. Her tone was steady, but her eyes searched his face like a map she hadn't read in years, afraid of what she'd find. But, she knew that look.

He nodded slowly. "Yeah," he said, stepping forward, jaw tight. "Can we talk for a second?"

She nodded back, slowly, buying herself time. She knew that tone. The one used when words were heavy and consequences inevitable. The voice of someone who had already made a decision and now needed the world to bend around it. She motioned toward the old oak table, its surface worn smooth by school projects and birthday candles long blown out.

"Of course, dear" she said, taking her seat across from him. Crossing her arms, bracing for what was coming next.

He lowered himself into the chair like it hurt. The light caught the amber in his eyes – his father's – and for a moment, she forgot to breathe. His jaw was set, the kind of serious that only surfaced when something mattered deeply.

"Mom," he began, his voice gentle but unwavering. "I've made a decision. But please – just hear me out. I'm joining the Army. I want to be a helicopter pilot."

The words didn't register. They floated, suspended in the stillness like dust motes. Then they dropped like stones – hard, fast, brutal.

"No," she said. Not loudly, but with a finality that startled even her. "Luke. No. Please tell me you're not serious. Do you understand what you're saying? What this means?"

"I do," he said, firmer now. "I've been thinking about it for a long time. It's not a whim. I've already signed the paperwork."

Her hands curled tight against the table's edge, anchoring herself to the earth that had just tilted beneath her. A chill slid down her spine. The kitchen, once warm, felt suddenly colder, as if the wind had shifted. She just stared at him.

"You've never flown a helicopter in your life," she said, the words tumbling out. "You don't know what that job does to people. To families. To me."

"Mom, I know about Dad," he said quietly. "And Uncle Edward."

Her brother's name shattered something deep inside her. Edward. And then she thought about his father, Luke Sr. The man she had loved with every piece of herself – gone before their son took his first breath. She remembered Hong Kong. The lights on the harbor. His hands in her hair. And then - the call that shattered her world. The folded flag. The bone-deep ache that never fully left.

"Then you know why I'm terrified," she said, her voice cracking. "You know what it did to this family. What it did to me when I - when we lost them both." Her voice broke, vision blurring.

All she could think of was Edward. Luke. And now her son. Her baby.

"I'm not him, Mom," he said gently. "I'm not Dad. I'm not trying to fill anyone's shoes. It's different now. I want to do something that matters. Something bigger than me."

"No," she snapped, louder now. "You don't get to say it's not the same. You weren't there. You didn't stand next to your mother at her son's grave. You didn't watch the love of your life lowered into the ground while carrying his child. You didn't bury two men and come home to a house that felt like a tomb."

He reached for her hand, but she pulled away. She rose slowly and crossed the kitchen, steps uneven, like the ground itself had shifted. At the window, she braced herself against the counter, staring out at the garden she had tended for twenty years. Shadows stretched across the grass. The old oak stood tall, its branches cradling the treehouse where her son once played.

"You don't understand, Luke. You can't. I gave this country my brother. I gave it the man I loved. And now you're telling me that's not enough? That it wants you too?"

He followed her, his footsteps careful, deliberate. He stood beside her, tall and still, resting a hand on her shoulder. It was a comfort. And an echo – Luke Sr. had once stood the same way.

"I'm not trying to replace them," he said softly. "I'm not trying to be Dad, or Uncle Edward. I'm just trying to be me. To serve. To fly. This is mine to choose."

She turned away, gripping the edge of the counter. The tears came then – hot, angry. She thought about how she had raised him to be brave and thoughtful. And now, for a moment she almost wished she hadn't. She wished he'd grown to be selfish. Cowardly. Anything but this.

"I'm not asking for permission," he said. "I'm asking for your blessing. For your belief in me. This is what I feel called to do."

"You are my whole world," she whispered, her voice breaking. "From the moment I first held you, I swore I would protect you. After everything, I promised myself nothing would ever take you from me."

"I know," he said behind her. "And you did. You gave me everything. But I'm not a boy anymore. I need to do this, Mom. I feel like I'm supposed to."

She turned to face him. Her cheeks were streaked with tears, her voice hoarse. "Then go," she said, trembling. "Do what you need to do. But don't ask me to pretend this doesn't rip me open. Don't ask me to smile and wave the flag like it doesn't cost me something I'll never get back."

Again she looked at him – really looked. The face she had memorized since the day he was born. The soul she had wrapped her heart around. His eyes held so much of his father – the same stubborn fire, the same quiet conviction.

"I may never be okay with it," she whispered. "Not really."

"I know."

"But I won't stop you. If this is what you feel you want to do, I'll support you. I won't stop loving you. I'll write you every week. And if you don't write me back, I'll call someone in Washington and make them track your ass down."

He laughed, tears forming in his own eyes. "I promise I'll write, Mom. I'll call whenever I can."

She stepped into his arms then, folding into him like a wave crashing against the shore. She held him the way she had when he was six and feverish, the way she did his father before he had died.

"I love you, Luke," she said, voice thick with grief and pride. "With everything I have."

"I love you too, Mom."

He kissed her forehead, the same way his father had. He turned toward the door. The screen creaked open, then closed with a thud that felt far too final.

Emily stood frozen, watching his silhouette cross the yard toward his truck. The sun caught his shoulders just right and for a moment – a single breath – he looked exactly like his father. Same walk. Same will. Clear as day.

She reached out and pressed her palm to the windowpane, her voice barely above a whisper. She prayed a prayer, "God… just keep him safe. I've already given too much. I couldn't survive losing him too."

The words hung in the air – fragile and fierce.

A mother's plea. A family's legacy. A prayer to whatever was listening.

Chapter Fifteen

Living and Giving

2:35 PM, CST; July 21, 1992, Tuesday
Smith/Jones Family Home
Galesburg, Illinois, USA

WEEKS HAD PASSED since Emily stood in the driveway, watching her son's truck disappear down the road. Pride and aching twisted inside her as she waved until the red taillights were swallowed by the horizon and dust returned to stillness. The silence that followed had a weight to it – a kind of hush that settled over the house like a winter fog, quiet but insistent, as though time itself had paused to grieve his absence.

The house hadn't changed, not really. The kitchen still welcomed the morning with warm light spilling through the curtains, the coffee maker still hissed and sputtered with familiar rhythm, birds still called from the dogwood trees. But something essential had gone with her son, Luke. Something sacred. The air felt thinner, the corners darker, the ticking of the clock louder – as if the house were holding its breath, waiting for someone who would not walk through the door for a long time.

Emily moved through the house like someone tracing the outlines of a memory. She smoothed the wrinkles in Luke's bedspread, straightened books he wouldn't read again for months. She sat on the porch swing long after the sun had set, watching the sky turn to velvet, the air growing cooler. Her ears strained for phantom footsteps, the soft thud of boots in the hallway. But the quiet held.

Grief, she was learning, didn't only come for the dead. It came for the living too, for change, for absence, for the passage of time you couldn't stop. Luke Jr. was alive, thriving, chasing his future in the sky, but she missed him with a bone-deep ache, a hollow space in her chest that no amount of time or distraction could fill. She had become so comfortable in her life, she had been able to see her son every few weeks while he was in college. And it wasn't just him. It was Edward, gone too soon, his memory now a sharp edge in her heart. It was Luke, a love unraveled by pain and years. It was the self she'd once been, the one she had pressed down in the name of motherhood and duty, survival, and the slow erosion of her own needs.

One restless afternoon, she found herself in the attic, sitting cross-legged on the floor surrounded by boxes she hadn't opened in years. She wasn't sure what she was looking for – maybe nothing at all – but her hands found something familiar: Edward's journal. The leather worn and warm with time. She opened it and read a passage she must've read a dozen times:

"Healing isn't forgetting. It's remembering with less fear."

She closed the book, pressing it to her chest, and exhaled. The words didn't sting like they once had. They felt like an invitation, a soft exhale in a room too long held tight.

That night, she and her husband, Richard, sat on the back porch, stars beginning to peek through the navy sky. The air was thick with cicadas and the sweet scent of jasmine. Richard had come into her life gently, a former high school classmate of her's and Edward's, steady and kind. He had stepped into the role of a father figure for young Luke without trying to replace the man who had come before. His love had been a balm in the years after the war – uncomplicated, enduring, a place she could finally rest.

"You've been quiet lately," Richard said gently, his hand covering hers on the armrest, his voice warm with concern.

"I miss him," she whispered, her words coming out thick with unshed tears.

"I know," he said quietly, his thumb brushing over the back of her hand. "I miss him too, but he is following his dreams."

"It's not just Luke Jr leaving. It's… everything. All the versions of myself I've left behind. I thought when he left, I'd feel proud. And I do. But there's this… emptiness. Like I don't know who I'm supposed to be now. I've spent my whole life folding myself into what others needed, but now I'm not sure what's left."

Richard nodded, his eyes deep and understanding. He didn't rush to fill the silence, which was one of the things she loved most about him. He sat with silence the way others filled it – with respect. "You don't have to know tonight," he said eventually, his voice steady. "But if there's something calling to you, Emily… I think you owe it to yourself to listen."

She turned to look at him, his face soft in the porch light. "I've been thinking about the VA Center. About going down there to volunteer."

His answer came without hesitation. "Then go."

She blinked, surprised by the ease of his response. "You think I should?"

"I think you've spent your whole life helping people. Maybe it's time to do it in a way that feeds your soul, too." He leaned closer, his voice low and encouraging. "You're not done yet, Emily. You've still got more to give."

*****

The next morning, Emily drove across town to the VA Center – a squat brick building shaded by towering oaks, their branches spread like watchful arms over the parking lot. Her heart thrummed against her ribs as she stepped inside, unsure of what she would say or where she would be needed. But by the end of the week, she was serving lunch in the cafeteria, wiping down tables, chatting with veterans who arrived alone and left with softened expressions.

And she kept going back. Each time, they gave her more to do – helping with mail, driving someone to a doctor's appointment, organizing a community outreach night. And then one day, when the usual coordinator had to leave early, they asked her to sit in on a grief support group.

She sat in the circle of folding chairs, just another person with a story. At first, she listened. Listened to a man who had lost his brother in Vietnam and still couldn't walk into a fireworks show without shaking. To a woman whose husband died by suicide two years after coming home from Iraq. To a father who hadn't spoken to his son in over a decade because neither knew how to say, "I'm sorry. For the demons that he brought home from deployment"

When Emily spoke, it wasn't with intent. The words came like breath. Soft. Honest. Real.

"I lost my brother and my son's father to the war," she said, her voice steady but tender. "For a long while, it seemed that I was cursed. Haunted by the same ghosts."

The room stilled. One man nodded slowly. A woman reached for a tissue. She hadn't planned to share, but it felt right. When the session ended, no one rushed to leave. A few lingered. One woman, eyes rimmed red, took Emily's hands in hers. "You get it," she said, her voice raw but grateful. Then she continued to help with the grief support groups.

Later that week, a counselor named Adrienne – mid-forties, sharp eyes softened by years of listening – approached Emily as she was stacking chairs.

"You ever think about doing this for real?" Adrienne asked, her tone curious, but with a spark of recognition.

Emily blinked. "What do you mean?"

"I mean you have a gift. You listen like someone who knows how heavy silence can be. You speak like someone who's walked through fire."

Emily smiled, a little embarrassed, but something inside her fluttered. "I've never studied counseling. I wouldn't know where to start."

Adrienne shrugged. "Then maybe it's time to find out. There are programs. Certifications. Even full degrees if that's what you want. I've seen people come through here with fancy diplomas and no empathy. But you – you've lived it. That is what really matters."

That night, she brought it up to Richard. He was at the sink, rinsing dishes, when she stepped into the kitchen and leaned against the doorframe. "What would you think," she began slowly, "if I went back to school?"

He turned off the water, wiped his hands on a dish towel, and turned to face her. "I'd think it's about damn time."

She laughed, startled. "Really?"

"You've spent years helping everyone else grieve. Maybe this is your path to healing too."

She took a few weeks to think about it. She searched online, scribbled down notes, weighed fears she hadn't felt since she was twenty. But in the end, she applied.

The first class was terrifying, like stepping onto a tightrope. She was twice the age of some of the others. Her hands trembled when she spoke. But when the lectures turned to trauma, to ambiguous loss, to the language of mourning, she felt something click into place. Not like she was learning something new – but remembering something she already knew in her bones.

Grief is a language, she came to understand. And she had learned to speak it fluently.

In time, Emily began to help run support groups more regularly – first at the VA Center, then at a community outreach space downtown. She helped people write letters they'd never send, light candles for anniversaries that no one else remembered. She sat with mothers who'd lost sons, spouses who couldn't sleep in their shared beds, veterans who woke up every night gasping for air.

And she never judged. Because she'd been there, too.

One night, after a particularly heavy session, a young man lingered behind. He had a sleeve tattoo of dog tags and dates and held his grief tight in his shoulders, his posture heavy with unsaid things.

"My brother died in Afghanistan," he said, his voice tight with guilt. "I wasn't there. I was supposed to be, but got reassigned at the last minute. I don't know how to stop blaming myself."

Emily looked at him gently, her gaze steady and calm. "You don't have to stop. Not today. Just try to carry it differently."

He nodded, tears thick in his lashes. "Thank you."

She watched him go, the door closing softly behind him, and realized she hadn't thought of her own pain in quite the same way since she'd begun this work. It hadn't disappeared. But like Adrienne had once told her, she had learned to carry it differently.

That night, she opened her journal – she still continued to write in journals since the first one she had started after Edward's death, the leather darker now, more worn. She flipped to a blank page.

Today, I saw the mirror of my younger self in a man half my age, choking on guilt he didn't deserve. And I knew what to say – not because I read it in a book, but because I've stood in that darkness and reached for the light. This work… it doesn't erase the past. But it redeems it, one voice at a time.

She closed the journal and looked out the window at the stars beginning to scatter across the dark sky. Her son was somewhere under the same blanket of stars, flying, becoming. And she – Emily – was becoming too.

And it felt, finally, like she wasn't just surviving anymore.

She was home. In herself. In her calling. In the stories she helped others tell.

And in the quiet, steady heartbeat of healing. She had a new purpose in life. One that would allow her to take her grief and help others express theirs and in some way both could find healing.

Chapter Sixteen

Old Wounds

4:00 PM, EST; April 17, 2003, Thursday
Vietnam Veterans Reunion
Washington, D.C., USA

YEARS HAD DULLED the sharpest edges of Emily's grief, but some wounds never truly healed – they simply changed form. The ache remained, folded into quiet moments: when she sorted laundry alone, when an old song drifted from a radio like a ghost from summers past, or when her son – Luke Edward Smith – tilted his head just so, in that contemplative way his father once did. He bore the names of two men he had never met: his father, Luke David Gentry, and his uncle Edward, Emily's twin. Each name carried the weight of memory, of legacy, of loss carved deep into her bones.

But nothing, not even all the years since the war had prepared her for the moment, almost three years ago now, when her son said the words she both feared and somehow expected:

"I want to serve, Mom. I want to fly."

He had just graduated college, commissioned as an officer, and stood in her kitchen like a man becoming, radiating purpose. Her breath had caught in her throat. The room, with its floral curtains and smell of cinnamon coffee, seemed to tilt beneath her. Fear surged through her like a tide, but so did pride. Cold and quiet and inescapable.

Luke had inherited his father's resolve and his uncle's sharpness. Now he was engaged to a girl Emily adored – a kind, clear-eyed young woman he met during his second year at university. And yet, even with this beautiful future unfolding, the past still curled around her heart. The thought of letting go again, even in a different way, twisted something deep inside her. Not grief exactly, but its twin.

Over time, Emily had found her way back to herself. She had gone back to school, slowly, tentatively, until her purpose sharpened. Counseling had saved her as much as she'd hoped to save others. Working with veterans and their families sitting beside their wounds, their silences, their unspeakable losses. It had given her grief a second life, one rooted in compassion rather than despair. At the VA, she had found something close to peace.

And yet, tonight, she stood far from that world, far from the rhythm of sessions and journals and home. The large reception hall of a national Vietnam veterans' convention stretched around her, pulsing with old stories, worn uniforms, and the kind of laughter that comes only from survival. She hadn't planned to come. But something an old dream, a gentle nudge from her soul. It had drawn her here.

She wore a simple black dress and a silver pin Luke Sr. had once given her when they were in Hong Kong. It was a small gift from a time before everything fractured. Her name badge read:

Emily Smith, Grief Counselor. Galesburg, IL

But she felt, in this space, more like a witness than anything else.

She moved through the room slowly, her heels clicking softly across polished tile, past tables lined with faded photographs, medals, and folded letters. Conversations rose around her – gravel-voiced reunions, the scent of bourbon and memory thick in the air.

Then she saw him.

He stood near a memorial display, his hand resting lightly on the corner of a photo frame. His back was turned, but she would have known him in any crowd, in any year. Reagan.

The last man to see Luke alive. His best friend. The one who had promised to bring him home, but didn't.

Her breath caught. The years had drawn silver through his hair and deepened the lines around his eyes, but the core of him – his bearing, his quiet intensity – remained. And in that instant, the noise around her fell away, like water draining from a basin. There was only the space between them.

She didn't remember crossing the room only the pull, that gravity of shared loss.

When Reagan turned and their eyes met, time collapsed. For a long moment, neither of them spoke.

"Emily," he said softly, her name breaking like glass against the hush.

"Reagan." Her voice trembled, but her smile came worn but genuine.

They stood still, caught in a moment that held decades. Then he stepped forward and folded her into a hug. Not the cautious embrace of old friends, but something fuller. The reunion of two people who had bled from the same wound.

When he pulled back, his hands lingered gently on her arms. "You look…" He paused, searching her face. "Like time's been kind."

She gave a quiet laugh and wiped at a tear she hadn't realized had fallen. "That's generous. But the years – well, I've learned to wear them like armor."

They found a quiet corner near a tall window, a little removed from the swell of conversation. For a while, they sat in companionable silence – the kind that didn't need to be filled. Then slowly, the words came.

Emily told him about her work. About counseling. The veterans. The stories. The ache and the beauty of bearing witness.

"At first," she said, "it felt like reopening the wound. But then I realized… helping others carry their pain made mine feel less like a solitary burden."

Reagan nodded, his gaze steady. "That sounds like something Luke would've admired. He always said you were the strongest person he knew."

She smiled softly. Then told him about her son – his accelerated college years, his pilot's wings, his engagement. "He's deployed now. In Afghanistan," she said, voice shaking. "And sometimes I wonder if history is circling back. Like it's trying to take something from me again."

Reagan leaned in, his expression tender but firm. "It's not the same war, Emily. Not the same world. And he's got you to guide him. That's more grounding than you think."

She studied him in the dim light. His eyes still held that fire tempered, wiser now, but intact.

"And you?" she asked. "What brought you here?"

"I come every few years. Mostly, I come here to listen." He paused. "I reconnected with a few of the guys from our unit at one of these reunions a while back. Luke's memory… it lives in them too. These reunions, they're the only time I don't have to explain."

She reached for his hand and held it. "I'm glad you came this year."

His fingers closed around hers, and something unspoken passed between them – recognition, forgiveness, maybe even grace.

As the evening waned and veterans trickled toward the exits, Emily introduced him to her husband, Richard – a kind, steady man who had never tried to step into Luke's shadow, only walk beside her in the life that remained.

Reagan shook his hand firmly, a flicker of relief in his expression. "You've got a good one here," he said to Richard.

"I know," Richard replied simply.

The two men exchanged a few quiet words about military life, about the strange mercy of second chances, about memory and how it refuses to fade.

Before they parted, Reagan turned to Emily once more and rested a hand gently on her shoulder.

"Take care of your boy," he said. "He's carrying a powerful legacy. But with you in his corner, that legacy won't break him. It'll shape him."

Her throat tightened. "Don't disappear again, Reagan. There's not many pieces of our past left. I don't want to lose another."

His smile was soft. "You won't lose me. I promise."

Outside, under a sky freckled with stars, Emily stepped onto the quiet street beside Richard. The air was cool and clean, and the buzz of the convention faded behind them like a dream slipping into dawn.

She looked up.

Luke was somewhere beneath that same sky. Flying. Becoming.

And she – Emily – was still becoming too.

Her grief no longer felt like a wound. It was something deeper now. A part of her. A part she had learned to carry, like a name, like a story passed down in whispers.

She closed her eyes and whispered to the stars – words she'd once spoken long ago after her boy had fallen asleep:

"Wherever you are, Luke… we're still here. We remember. We love you."

And this time, when she said it, she felt it in her marrow:

He heard her.

Chapter Seventeen

Echoes of First Steps

9:23 AM, CST; June 5, 2008, Tuesday
Smith Family Home
Montgomery, Alabama, USA

THE RISING SUN SPILLED golden light across the old VW van's dashboard, casting shadows over the cracked leather and faded maps scattered on the passenger seat. Milly, now nearly five decades old, still purred like a cat under Emily Smith's careful touch. It had been tough at first – more than once she'd considered trading her in – but over the years, Emily had become quite the mechanic. She'd kept the van running all this time, the same way she'd kept her memories – well-oiled, treasured, and stubbornly intact. The van bore its years with a kind of pride: a rusted bumper, mismatched hubcaps, stories etched into every scratch.

Emily, now in her seventies, was smaller and a little more stooped than she had been on that first journey west all those years ago. But her eyes still carried the same spark – the same restless fire that had once taken her from Illinois to San Francisco and beyond. She adjusted the rearview mirror, catching sight of Rebecca curled up in the passenger seat, one foot on the dash, earbuds in, and eyes closed.

Rebecca was fourteen. Almost fifteen. Too tall for her own good, sharp-tongued but sweet-hearted, and very much her father's daughter – and his mother's granddaughter. There was something in the set of her jaw, the way she asked questions without flinching, that reminded Emily of herself at that age. She had picked her up two days ago from

Luke's house in Alabama. It had been years since they'd had more than a weekend together, but this summer was different. This was the summer Rebecca asked to come with her. And not just for a few days. For the whole trip.

Emily smiled to herself. She hadn't said yes immediately. She'd waited – wanted to be sure it was what Rebecca really wanted, not just a whim or teenage escape. She remembered the way Rebecca had stood in her living room, serious as a heartbeat, holding the journal in both hands.

"I want to see the places you saw during that summer," she'd said. "The ones you wrote about."

Emily had never spoken much about the journal, but she knew instantly which summer Rebecca was referring to by the way she emphasized the word "that." The journal had traveled with her on that first pilgrimage west – pages filled with grief, stories, letters to her twin brother, Edward, and even a few to the man, her biological grandfather, she'd loved and lost, Luke. Over the years, the journal had grown: more trips, more memories, more miles. It became a kind of map of her inner world – filled with letters to people she still missed, thoughts about the world, fears she could never say aloud. She never meant for anyone to read it.

But one day, Rebecca had found it.

She hadn't asked permission. She'd found it tucked in a box of road maps and vintage postcards in Emily's attic over the previous spring break, shortly after Emily's husband Richard passed. When she handed it back, she said simply, "You wrote like you knew what I'd need."

Oddly, Emily wasn't upset. And that was that. From then on, Rebecca had been begging her grandmother to take her on one of those famous trips.

Now, somewhere on a two-lane highway slicing through Kansas wheat fields, Emily shifted gears and gently nudged Milly west. The old van rumbled faithfully beneath her hands. Rebecca stirred beside her, stretching like a cat.

"You hungry?" Emily asked.

Rebecca pulled out one earbud. "Starving."

They found a diner with checkered floors and orange vinyl booths. The kind of place with waitresses named Doris and bottomless coffee.

A bell jingled when they walked in. It smelled like syrup and bacon and decades of stories. Rebecca ordered pancakes the size of hubcaps. Emily stuck with eggs and grits.

"So," Rebecca said between bites, "did you really get stuck in Death Valley once?"

Emily laughed. "Twice, actually. First time, I ran out of gas. Second time, I ran out of patience."

Rebecca grinned. "It's in the journal."

"You read that far?"

"I read it all. Twice."

Emily sat back, folding her arms. "And?"

"It made me cry. And laugh. And… I don't know. I guess I just didn't know you were ever young."

Emily raised her eyebrows. "Thanks."

"No, I mean – you were brave. And lonely. But not alone. It's weird. I feel like I know Uncle Edward now. And Granddad."

Emily paused. It was the first time Rebecca – or anyone – had ever referred to Luke as Granddad. The names hung in the air, gentle but heavy. Emily reached for her coffee. "They were both part of me. Still are."

"Do you think about them every day?"

Emily nodded. "Every road I've ever taken, they've ridden along."

Back on the highway, they played music from both their playlists – Fleetwood Mac and Phoebe Bridgers, Simon & Garfunkel and Taylor Swift. Rebecca napped again, arms crossed, the rise and fall of her breath syncing with the rhythm of the road. Emily drove in silence, remembering.

She remembered the night she wrote her first letter to Edward, camping in the Rockies, heart torn wide open by the weight of absence. She remembered the gas station in Arizona where a stranger gave her free oil and a quiet blessing. She remembered the Golden Gate Bridge, where she cried for three hours and then promised to live for them both.

Then she remembered the Marine who had stolen her heart. Luke Senior. She remembered picking him and his friend up on the side of a road so many years ago. She remembered their time in Hong Kong, the shared laughter, the softest moments in hard places. But mostly, she remembered the way he made her feel – seen, cherished, real.

And, finally, she remembered her son, Luke – her miracle child, born when she thought she might never find love again. He had her eyes and his father's laugh. Raising him had been her greatest adventure. Every decision had been a prayer for his safety, every milestone a whispered thank-you to the ones who never made it home.

That night, they camped in a park near the Colorado border. Emily built the fire; Rebecca set up the chairs. They ate roasted marshmallows and watched the stars bloom over the sky like wildflowers. The scent of pine mixed with the smoke, and somewhere in the distance, an owl called out.

"I want to learn to drive," Rebecca said suddenly.

Emily blinked. "Now?"

"Not this second. I just… you know. I'm almost fifteen. Thought you could teach me."

Emily studied her granddaughter's face. So eager and full of life. So vulnerable. She saw a little of herself there, and a little of Edward, and so much of the boy she raised.

"I'd be honored."

Rebecca smiled and kicked off her sneakers, curling her toes in the dirt. "Do you think the past changes? Like, when we remember it differently?"

Emily tossed another log on the fire. "I think memory is like a road. Sometimes straight. Sometimes winding. But the journey it takes you on – that's the part that stays true."

Rebecca chewed on that. "You know what part of the journal I liked most?"

Emily shook her head.

"The letter you wrote to your future granddaughter. You didn't even know if you'd have one. But you said if you did, you'd want her to live wild and kind and bold."

Emily's throat caught. She'd forgotten that letter. She had written it one late night outside Flagstaff, the wind whipping against the tent, her future nothing but a blur of maybes.

"I'm trying," Rebecca whispered.

Emily reached over and took her hand. "You already are."

They sat like that for a long while, hands warm, fire crackling, stars overhead, and Milly parked in the background like an old faithful friend.

The next morning, they found an empty parking lot off the highway. Rebecca climbed into the driver's seat of the VW, nerves buzzing.

"Easy on the clutch," Emily said. "And trust the feel of the road."

Rebecca stalled twice. Laughed. Tried again.

By the third try, she rolled the van forward, lurching slightly but still moving. She whooped with joy. Emily whooped louder.

They kept going – across plains, through mountains, down old highways and up winding passes. At every overlook, they read a letter from the journal. Some were sad. Some hilarious. One was a list of things Emily wanted to do before she turned thirty – half were crossed off, half weren't. At one scenic rest stop, they drew their own map on the back of a napkin, marking places they'd been and ones they still hoped to see.

At another, Rebecca wrote her own letter and added it to the back.

"To the girl I'll be when I'm your age," she wrote. "Don't forget this trip. Don't forget how brave Grandma was. How scared I was. How we laughed. How we loved. And how it all started with a van and a journal."

The last stop of the journey was the Pacific. Just like Emily's first trip.

Rebecca stood barefoot in the surf, arms spread wide. Emily stood behind her, hair wind-whipped, heart full. The waves pulled back, rolled in again, repeating like memory.

"I get it now," Rebecca said.

"Get what?"

"Why you never really stopped driving."

Emily smiled. "Because the road never ends. It just changes directions."

They stayed a few more days in California before heading back east, slowly. Emily let Rebecca drive more and more. Let her make wrong turns down one-way streets. Let her find new paths. It was part of the legacy now.

Weeks later, when they pulled back into Luke's driveway, the sun was rising again, just like it had at the start.

Luke came out and wrapped his mother in a long hug. Then he kissed Rebecca's forehead.

"You take good care of her?" he asked.

"She took care of me," Rebecca laughed.

That night, before bed, Emily found the journal gently sitting on her pillow. Rebecca had added her own pages, careful and ink-stained.

And tucked between two old pages was a photograph – Rebecca, standing in the Pacific surf, arms outstretched, wind in her hair.

Emily stared at it a long while.

Then, gently, she slipped it into the back of the journal.

The road would call again. Maybe not soon. Maybe not far. But when it did, Emily knew she wouldn't go alone.

She never had. And she never would again – because much like life, the road never ends; it just changes direction.

EPILOGUE

Next Chapters

3:35 PM, CST; August 27, 2008, Wednesday
State Route 61
Tunica, MS, USA

THE ROAD BACK HOME STRETCHED like a winding thread across the South – familiar in rhythm, but different now. Emily had dropped off her granddaughter, Rebecca, in Alabama after their week-long trip, and now Milly – with her stubborn hum – rolled solo down quiet highways. The wheels turned beneath her like time itself, pulling her from one chapter toward another. It was supposed to be a straight shot home, but something tugged at her: a name she'd seen in a museum pamphlet weeks ago for Jerome, Arkansas.

She didn't know why it lingered. Maybe it was the reverence in the docent's voice, or how Rebecca had asked questions after watching an old documentary in a hotel room. Emily hadn't known how to answer then, but as the Arkansas road signs multiplied, she felt now might be the time to learn.

The landscape changed subtly – flat, green, and expansive as she entered the Mississippi River Delta. Jerome, a blink-and-you-miss-it town, had once held one of ten War Relocation Centers during World War II. Over 8,000 Japanese Americans, many U.S. citizens, were incarcerated there. Emily had never studied it in school. It wasn't in Edward's journals or Luke's stories. Still, something told her it mattered.

She turned onto a gravel road leading to the former Jerome camp. The original buildings were gone - no barracks, no barbed wire – but a sun-bleached historical marker stood near a quiet cotton field. Emily stepped from the van, wind tugging at her sleeves. She walked to the marker, brushing her fingers over the bronze letters.

"Here stood the Jerome War Relocation Center," it read. "From October 6, 1942, to June 30, 1944, thousands of Japanese Americans were unjustly detained here."

A tightness rose in her chest. The sorrow hit harder than expected, echoing the ache she'd felt when reading Reagan's letter about Luke. These lives, uprooted and silenced, were part of a history nearly forgotten.

A weathered bench sat beside the marker, half-hidden by tall grass. Emily sat, letting the silence settle. She pictured children in makeshift classrooms, mothers hanging laundry, fathers coaxing gardens from unfamiliar soil. She imagined the fear – and the resilience.

Her thoughts drifted to Luke.

From her bag, she pulled the leather-bound journal she'd begun after Edward died. She opened to a blank page and wrote:

"I didn't know about Jerome. Not really. Not until today. I think of the families who passed through here, unsure of what lay ahead. How the American dream must have looked like a mirage behind barbed wire."

The wind stirred across the field, whispering like long-silenced voices.

Then a voice interrupted: "Most folks don't stop here."

Emily looked up. An elderly man stood nearby, binoculars in hand, a faded Army cap on his head. He nodded toward the marker. "It's good you did."

She stood. "I didn't mean to trespass."

He waved her off. "You're not. This land used to belong to a friend. He gave it to the state to preserve the memory." He looked out over the fields. "They called it 'relocation,' but it was imprisonment."

"I didn't learn much about it growing up," Emily said.

"Most don't. My wife's parents were here. Came from California to grow rice. Lost everything. I was born here." He held out a hand. "Hiroshi Takeda. Call me Hiro."

"Emily Smith," she replied, shaking his hand.

He sat beside her. "My father fought with the 442nd Infantry Regiment. You ever heard of them?"

She shook her head.

"Japanese Americans. They volunteered while their families were behind fences. Most decorated unit in U.S. history." His voice was steady, but fierce. "My uncle died in Italy. Never saw his parents again."

Emily blinked back tears. "I'm so sorry."

"Don't be. Just remember them."

They sat quietly as birds called from distant trees. Emily thought of Edward, of Luke, of all the stories never told.

Hiro stood. "You should meet my wife. She runs a small center up the road. Keeps records, photos, and letters. Come by before you leave town."

"I will," she said.

He tipped his cap. "Safe travels, Emily Smith."

She watched him walk away, then sat back down, overwhelmed. The strength and sorrow of this place mattered. And someone had to carry it forward.

Emily drove to the center – a modest building with a weathered sign: Jerome Remembrance House. Inside, a woman in her seventies greeted her.

"You must be Emily. I'm Aiko. Hiro called ahead."

The center held photos, letters, and artifacts: families outside barracks, children in schoolrooms, soldiers in uniform. Aiko led her through the exhibits, gently sharing names and stories. Families who returned to nothing. Soldiers who earned medals while their mothers lived in shacks.

One photo stopped Emily: a young woman, not much older than herself with Luke, holding a baby in front of a barrack marked "12-C."

"That's my mother," Aiko said. "She gave birth to me here in 1943."

"You were born here?" Emily asked softly.

Aiko nodded. "And I built this place to make sure people didn't forget. Because forgetting means it can happen again."

Later, before Emily left, Aiko handed her a small envelope. "A letter from my mother. She wrote it the day the camp closed. Maybe it'll help you finish your journey."

Emily read it hours later, twilight falling. The letter, in delicate script, held both longing and quiet strength:

"We leave this place behind, but it will never leave us. The desert has held our tears, our laughter, our fears. But we also found strength. We endured. And in doing so, we became unbreakable."

She pressed the letter to her chest.

She knew now – she had another story to tell.

Emily didn't leave Jerome right away. As the sun bathed the fields in amber, she parked Milly beneath a sweetgum tree near the old site. She reached for her journal – the one she'd kept since Edward's death. This page, she knew, wasn't for her. It was for Rebecca.

She opened to a blank page and began.

Rebecca, many years down the road -

By the time you read this, I hope you'll be older than I was when I started this journey. I hope you'll be wiser. I hope you'll have loved deeply, lost a little, and learned to sit still with both joy and sorrow.

We've talked—on porches, in cars—about war, about family, about the past. But there were things I never found the words to say. Until now.

I just left a quiet field in Jerome, Arkansas. It doesn't look like much. But during World War II, thousands of Americans were imprisoned there—not for what they did, but for who they were.

I met a man whose father fought for this country while his family lived behind fences. I met a woman born in those barracks who built a center so no one would forget. They reminded me of something I've held close since the war took Luke and Edward: we don't honor the dead by forgetting the pain. We honor them by carrying it—and building something better.

Grief is strange. It changes shape. Sometimes it's thunder, sometimes a whisper. But it doesn't vanish. That's not its job. It reminds us we loved deeply.

This trip with you - it began as a distraction. But it became a walk through memory, through sacrifice and love. It taught me stories matter. Yours. Mine. All of them.

You once asked if I still miss them—Edward and Luke, your grandfather. The answer is yes. Every day. But missing them doesn't mean being lost. It means they lived so well, the world feels quieter without them.

But they aren't really gone.

I see them in your smile. I hear them in your questions. I feel them in the way you held my hand at the cemetery in Kansas, and in the way you sing when you think no one hears.

You come from people who endured. Who carried shame and found grace. Who rebuilt. You are not alone in your story.

So carry this with you: You are the legacy of love that didn't quit. The echo of sacrifices made in silence. The dream of those who never saw you bloom. And you can remember, retell, and redeem.

Don't fear the past. Learn from it. Speak it. Grow from it.

And when the world feels dark, when the road bends unexpectedly—find a quiet place. Write. Cry. Laugh. Feel it all. Then rise. Carry their names and keep walking.

Because that's what we do. We remember. We love. We live.

With all my love,

Grandmom Emily

Emily closed the journal and sat in the stillness. She tucked the letter behind the strap, knowing Rebecca wouldn't find it today or maybe not for many years. But she would. When she needed it.

The stars emerged in the twilight. Emily looked up, imagining Edward, Luke – all of them – watching too.

She turned Milly toward home, toward the next unwritten chapter.

And as the engine rumbled to life, Emily smiled.

Some journeys never really end. They just pass their story on.

Check Other Titles by Joseph Wainwright

Wheels of Brotherhood

Upcoming Titles by Joseph Wainwright

Men of Color – coming 2026

About the Author

Joseph Wainwright grew up in a small town in South Georgia. After high school, he attended college and graduated with a degree in Agriculture. After the attacks on the World Trade Centers in September 2001, he joined the United States Military, where he has currently served over 20 years. He is a lifelong student of military history, science, and various wars and battles. He currently resides in western Tennessee, where he enjoys spending time with his family visiting National Parks Sites, especially those that have military or cultural significance.

Note from the author:

Thank you very much for reading my novel. If you enjoyed the novel, please stop by Amazon and leave a review. Also, you can go to my website to get updates on upcoming novels, release dates, and/or follow my blog posts at https://josephwainwright11.wixsite.com/wheels.

www.ingramcontent.com/pod-product-compliance
Lightning Source LLC
LaVergne TN
LVHW010932110826
845149LV00013B/2568
* 9 7 9 8 9 9 0 2 0 9 6 1 9 *